COLLECTIVE *Biographies*

Women Scientists and Inventors

Toney Allman

ReferencePoint Press®

San Diego, CA

ReferencePoint Press®

Printed in the United States

For more information, contact:
ReferencePoint Press, Inc.
PO Box 27779
San Diego, CA 92198
www. ReferencePointPress.com

LIBRARY OF CONGRESS CATALOGING-IN-PUBLICATION DATA

Names: Allman, Toney.
Title: Women scientists and inventors / by Toney Allman.
Description: San Diego, CA : ReferencePoint Press, Inc., 2017. | Series: Collective biographies | Audience: Grade 9 to 12.- | Includes bibliographical references and index.
Identifiers: LCCN 2015050839 (print) | LCCN 2016009487 (ebook) | ISBN 9781682820322 (hardback) | ISBN 9781682820339 (epub)
Subjects: LCSH: Women scientists--Biography--Juvenile literature.
Classification: LCC Q141 .A455 2017 (print) | LCC Q141 (ebook) | DDC 509.2/52--dc23
LC record available at http://lccn.loc.gov/2015050839

CONTENTS

INTRODUCTION

Awe-Inspiring Contributions

Many women have made important and significant contributions to science, but few people can name a woman scientist except perhaps for Marie Curie, for her pioneering work in radioactivity. The reasons for this lack of familiarity with women's scientific discoveries and inventions are many. Throughout much of history women had to fight the prevalent prejudice against them as having minds unfit for higher education, especially in math and science. Young women were often barred from college because it was seen as unhealthy and unnatural for them. Under such circumstances, women's contributions were undervalued or unrecognized, even when they were able to acquire the education readily available to men. Legal barriers also presented problems. Married women had few rights and could not lawfully own property even into the nineteenth century. This meant that patenting an invention was impossible, so women had to acquire patents in their husbands' names. It is not surprising, then, that such women are not credited for their discoveries.

Not Quite Equal

Opportunities for women in science expanded dramatically as educational fairness and equal rights became the norm, notably toward the end of the nineteenth century. Yet even into the twentieth century prejudice against women—particularly in academia, where most highly regarded research takes place—existed. Women had to make names for themselves while working outside of traditional academic areas. "Indeed, the most well-known women scientists of the twentieth century were not members of any academic faculty,"[1] write Rosalind Chait Barnett and Laura Sabbatini of Brandeis University. The anthropologist Margaret Mead, for example, did not work for a university but for the American Museum of Natural History. She became an assistant curator there after her study expeditions to Samoa and New Guinea transformed the way anthropologists viewed cultural effects on human behavior. Rachel Carson, the zoologist and ecologist who essentially began the environmental conservation movement, worked for the US Fish and Wildlife Service as a writer and later supported herself by writing popular books about the dangers of fertilizers and pesticides. Barbara McClintock was a cytogeneticist who eventually won the 1983 Nobel Prize in Physiology or Medicine for her genetic discoveries, but she was denied tenure at the University of Missouri. She had to leave the academic world to work at Cold Spring Harbor Laboratory, a private research institution, in order to accomplish her research goals.

In other instances, women scientists who worked in collaboration with men found their contributions ignored in the larger world—as if only the male scientists had done the research. Chien-Shiung Wu, for example, was a brilliant nuclear physicist. In 1956, while at Columbia University, she and two male colleagues—Tsung-Dao Lee and Chen-Ning Yang—were researching the way in which nuclear particles behave. Lee and Yang proposed a hypothesis that an accepted law of nuclear particle emission was wrong. Wu designed and performed an experiment proving that assertion. In 1957 Lee and Yang won the Nobel Prize in Physics for the discovery, but Wu was omitted from consideration for the award. Rosalind Franklin, an English biochemist who did much of the research and discovery on the structure of the DNA molecule, was also denied recognition and

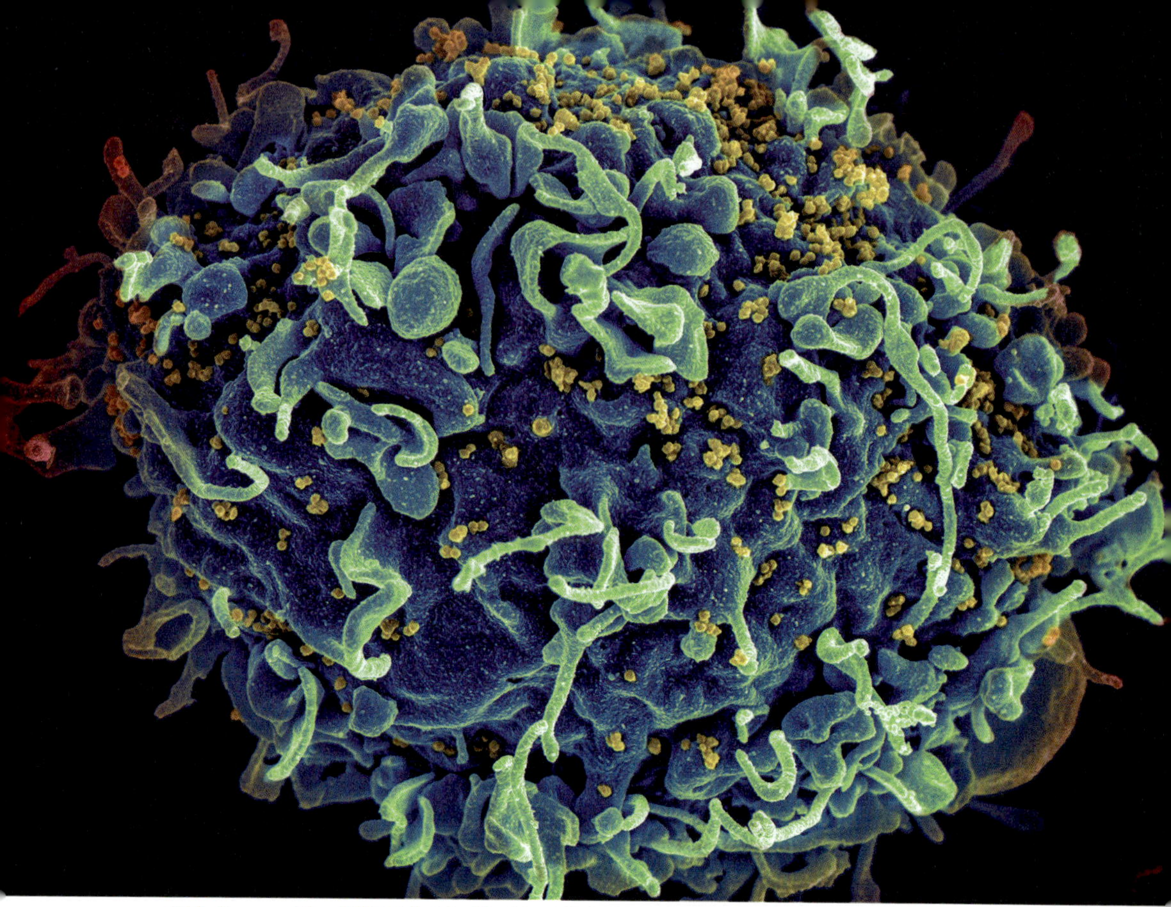

This human T-cell (highlighted in blue) is infected by HIV (highlighted in yellow). Françoise Barré-Sinoussi won the 2008 Nobel Prize in Physiology or Medicine as the codiscoverer of HIV.

a Nobel Prize. Without her knowledge, a male colleague, Maurice Wilkins, sent her results to James Watson and Francis Crick, who used her data to complete their work on the DNA helix and publish their results before she published hers. Watson, Crick, and Wilkins won the 1962 Nobel Prize in Physiology or Medicine.

Admirable Success

Despite such unfairness and discrimination, women scientists generally love their work and find the struggle worthwhile. Wu once said, "There is only one thing worse than coming home from the lab to a sink full of dirty dishes, and that is not going to the lab at all!"[2] Dedicated women have succeeded in science and rightfully deserve both fame and the world's respect and gratitude. In modern times, women noted for their achievements include, for instance, Françoise Barré-Sinoussi. In 2008 she won the Nobel Prize in Physiology or Medicine as the codiscoverer of HIV (the retrovirus responsible for AIDS). Gertrude B. Elion developed several important drug treatments, including AZT (the first drug to successfully treat AIDS). She jointly won the Nobel Prize in Physiology or Medicine in 1988. And Sally Ride, known mostly as an astronaut and the first American woman in orbit, was also a physicist, working on NASA programs such as deploying satellites and conducting other experiments and scientific observations in space. All of these women—along with many thousands of others throughout the world—had different areas of interest and worked in various fields of study, but all have in common a passion for knowledge and discovery and a dedication to science for its own sake.

> **"There is only one thing worse than coming home from the lab to a sink full of dirty dishes, and that is not going to the lab at all!"[2]**
>
> *—Chien-Shiung Wu, female nuclear physicist.*

CHAPTER 1

Lise Meitner

Lise Meitner, who was destined to become a pioneer in nuclear physics, was born on November 7, 1878, in Vienna, Austria, the third of eight children. Her parents were Jewish, although not religious, and both were believers in intellectual freedom and education. Early in life Lise showed an aptitude for and interest in mathematics and science, but her formal education ended when she was thirteen years old. High school and college educations were not available to girls during Lise's childhood. Undaunted, she began studying on her own, and her father encouraged and privately tutored her. Lise's parents also provided her with piano lessons, and she developed a lifelong love of music. Then, in 1897, the Austrian government opened its universities to women. Lise and her older sister, Gisela, began studying in earnest for university entrance examinations. Gisela passed first and entered medical school in 1900. In 1901, when she was twenty-three years old, Lise passed as well and entered the University of Vienna. In later years Lise Meitner always credited her parents for her chance to study science. She wrote, "Even today I am filled with deep gratitude for the unusual goodness of my parents, and the extraordinarily stimulating intellectual atmosphere in which my sisters and brothers and I grew up."[3]

For the Love of Physics

Meitner fell in love with physics as a course of study, but university life was not easy for her. She was painfully shy and intimidated by her inexperience in classroom work in comparison to the male students. In addition, physics was such a new scientific discipline that no one could imagine how to make a career out of it. At that time, scientists still argued over whether atoms really existed and whether they were indivisible or made up of subatomic particles. Nevertheless, Meitner saw physics as the pathway to understanding the truth of the world, and she persevered. By 1906 she received her doctoral degree in physics, only the second woman to do so at the University of Vienna. She could not teach at any university because no woman had ever done so, and no women's colleges existed in Austria either. She wrote to Marie Curie in Paris to ask for a position in her laboratory, but there were no openings available. Meitner found work teaching at a girls' school during the day; she pursued physics research on her own at night. Then, in 1907, she decided to travel to Berlin, where most physics research was taking place. Her parents gave her an allowance so that she could afford her living expenses in this venture.

No German universities at the time admitted women, but Meitner asked the great theoretical physicist Max Planck to let her audit his lectures at the University of Berlin, and he agreed. Planck was the originator of quantum theory, which explains the behavior of matter and energy at the atomic and subatomic levels and mathematically demonstrates that radiant energy exists in individual units called quanta. Meitner also came into contact with the head of the experimental physics institute at the University of Berlin, Professor Heinrich Rubens, and a young radiochemist named Otto Hahn, who sometimes worked with colleagues at the physics laboratories because of his interest in radiation. Rubens offered Meitner a position in his laboratory where she could collaborate on experiments with Hahn, who was close to her in age. Although the position was unpaid, Rubens's physics laboratory was welcoming to the young woman. She was accepted into the group of enthusiastic, youthful physicists (including Albert Einstein) who were absorbed in learning all they could about the revolutionary new discipline. The directors of the chemistry institute, where Hahn was officially employed as a chemist, were not accepting at all. Hahn had a basement room there where he was performing experiments with radiation measurements with different elements. Meitner was allowed to enter the basement lab through the basement door but forbidden to enter any other part of the institute, not even Hahn's chemistry laboratory upstairs. She was not allowed to have her own keys to the lab. To use the bathroom, Meitner had to leave the basement and walk to a public restaurant. Nevertheless, Meitner and

In 1907 Lise Meitner traveled to Germany, where she was offered an unpaid position at the experimental physics institute at the University of Berlin.

Hahn established a working relationship and a close friendship that endured for the next thirty years.

During this time physicists were rapidly developing a theory of the atom and radiation. Atoms are made up of a nucleus containing protons and neutrons (not identified until 1932), with electrons in orbit around the nucleus. Protons have a positive charge, electrons have a negative charge, and neutrons are neutral, with no charge. The attraction between protons and electrons holds the atom together, and neutrons help bind together the protons in the nucleus. The number of protons determines what element the atom is. For example, hydrogen has one proton and no neutrons, and aluminum has thirteen protons and fourteen neutrons. The atoms of many elements come in different forms with different numbers of neutrons in their nuclei. These different forms are called isotopes. Most atoms are in balance and stable, but the atoms in the isotopes of some elements are not. Unstable atoms try to become stable by emitting subatomic particles or energy. This is known as ionizing radiation. The four main types of nuclear radiation are alpha particles (two neutrons and two protons), beta particles (electrons), gamma rays (high-energy waves), and neutron particles (neutrons released through nuclear fission).

> "I love physics with all my heart. I can hardly imagine it not being part of my life."[4]
>
> *—Lise Meitner*

Real Research Opportunities

Meitner and Hahn developed techniques for studying alpha and beta radiation processes and the rate at which different isotopes lose their energy, or decay. It was exciting research, and Meitner wrote to a friend, "I love physics with all my heart. I can hardly imagine it not being part of my life."[4] Meitner's financial life also improved during this time. Planck hired her as his assistant. Then Hahn and eventually Meitner were appointed to paid positions at the new Kaiser Wilhelm Institute outside of Berlin. Their work on radioactivity was interrupted in 1914 by the start of World War I, however. Hahn joined the army, and Meitner volunteered as an X-ray technician in field hospitals. In 1917, back at the institute and in correspondence with Hahn (who was still in the military), Meitner performed work that led to the discovery of a new radioactive element—protactinium. In the scientific paper announcing the discovery, Meitner generously listed Hahn as the senior author and herself second, perhaps in deference to his military service.

After the war ended in 1918, Hahn became the director of the Kaiser Wilhelm Institute for Chemistry, and Meitner ran the Physics Department there, teaching physics and quantum mechanics. Through the 1920s and 1930s, Meitner continued her research—often in collaboration with Hahn—concentrating on the nucleus of the atom, or nuclear physics, with particular focus on the behavior of uranium. When Adolf Hitler and the Nazi Party came to power in Germany in 1933, the escalating rampant anti-Semitism and brutal racist policies against Jews made the country a dangerous place for Meitner, although she had converted to Christianity long before. Germans wanted only so-called Aryan physics taught in their universities, although there was no such thing. Einstein and many other German Jewish scientists were denounced and subsequently fled the Nazis. In 1937 a rabid Nazi scientist at the Kaiser Wilhelm Institute, Kurt Hess, denounced Meitner, saying, "The Jewess endangers the Institute."[5] In March 1938 Germany annexed Austria, making Meitner a German citizen and finally forcing her to flee as well. She was fifty-nine years old.

> "The Jewess endangers the Institute."[5]
>
> *—Nazi Kurt Hess, denouncing Lise Meitner.*

The World-Changing Discovery

In the middle of her most important experiments with Hahn, Meitner escaped to Stockholm, Sweden, where her favorite nephew, the physicist Otto Robert Frisch, was living. Meitner and Hahn continued their nuclear research through correspondence and secret meetings. In December 1938 Hahn and his assistant Fritz Strassman wrote to her about a strange experimental result—

A Narrow Escape

When Lise Meitner fled Nazi Germany for Stockholm, Sweden, in July 1938, very few people knew that she was not planning to return. The Nazi government sought to prevent such escapes and would later shut them down completely. Meitner pretended to be going on a vacation. She left most of her possessions in her apartment; her lab coat still hung on its hook at the institute; and experiments were left incomplete. But she had left just in time. In August the minister of education sent the institute's director a formal and ominous letter preparatory to Meitner's dismissal. It read, in part, "Frau Professor Lise Meitner, formerly an Austrian national, is working as a guest at the Kaiser Wilhelm Institute for Chemistry. In so far as the above-named has become a German national through the Anschluss of Austria, it must be certified what fraction of Jewish blood she possesses. . . . I request an expeditious response in this matter."

Quoted in Ruth Lewin Sime, *Lise Meitner: A Life in Physics.* Berkeley and Los Angeles: University of California Press, 1996, p. 210.

their uranium had seemed to burst and turn into barium when the nuclei were bombarded by neutrons. Could Meitner explain this weird, seemingly chemical reaction in terms of physics? With Frisch's assistance, Meitner figured out what had happened mathematically: the uranium nuclei had been split—a feat thought impossible by many. She named the process *nuclear fission* and published an article in 1939, describing the process and the energy it theoretically could release.

The renowned physicist Niels Bohr confirmed Meitner's theory with experiments of his own and gave her credit for it, but Hahn claimed the discovery for his own and published the results without ever mentioning her name. As a patriotic German national, Hahn could not admit that he had worked with a Jew or that she deserved any credit for his "German" discovery. Einstein, who had immigrated to America, feared the Nazis would use the knowledge of fission to build a weapon. He understood the importance of Meitner's nuclear fission immediately and, through President Franklin D. Roosevelt, initiated the US Manhattan Project. That project eventually led to the development of the atomic bomb. Hahn was awarded the Nobel Prize in

1944 for the discovery of fission, but Meitner was completely excluded.

In the physics community, at least, Meitner's extraordinary talents and contributions were understood. She had recognized and named nuclear fission and had calculated its energy release. In 1943 she and her nephew were invited to Los Alamos, New Mexico, to work on the atomic bomb. Frisch accepted, but Meitner was appalled at putting her physics to military use. She said, "I will have nothing to do with a bomb!"[6] When she learned that the first atomic bomb had been dropped on Hiroshima, Japan, in 1945, ending World War II, she was horrified and sickened. She walked alone in the woods for hours, trying to accept what had happened.

> "I will have nothing to do with a bomb!"[6]
>
> —*Lise Meitner*

Acclaim and Sorrow

Even though she had nothing to do with developing the bomb, Meitner was credited in the West with having uncovered the secrets of atomic fission and making the atomic bomb possible. News reporters wrote stories about her. Former First Lady Eleanor Roosevelt interviewed her for American radio. In 1946 she made her first visit to the United States to see two sisters who had immigrated to New York and Washington and Frisch, who was still at Los Alamos. On her arrival she was hailed as a hero by the press and the public and dubbed the "Jewish mother of the bomb."[7] The Women's National Press Club named her their Woman of the Year and feted her with a banquet during which she met President Harry Truman. She returned to Sweden as a celebrity but she felt like an exile with no country to call her own. She also worried about how nuclear fission would be used in the future.

Meitner never returned to Germany to live, although she visited several times. Her old feelings of closeness and trust with the scientists at the institute were irreparably damaged. Many German scientists, although not members of the Nazi Party, were nationalists. Meitner could not get over the apparent de-

Lise Meitner visited the United States in 1946. Although Meitner was credited with having uncovered the secrets of atomic fission, she worried about how that knowledge would be used in the future.

nial of responsibility and lack of remorse in the scientific community for the Nazism that had caused so much horror. Hahn complained, for instance, that Germany was being mistreated and that its people were being blamed for something in which they had not participated. He seemed to feel no guilt for never having resisted Nazi ideology and atrocities. Meitner knew how many scientists had silently gone along with Nazi beliefs of Aryan superiority and prejudice against all other races. She wrote in a letter to a friend, "If the best Germans do not understand now what has happened and what must never happen again, who should instruct young people that the path that was tried was tragic for Germany and the world?"[8] Yet she continued to treat her former colleagues kindly and with friendship, even writing letters on their behalf after the war to attest that they were

From Fission to Bomb

By the end of 1939 dozens of physicists had confirmed that Lise Meitner's nuclear fission was real and that the uranium atom's nucleus could be bombarded and split. Furthermore, in a chain reaction, such fission would result in the release of an unimaginable amount of energy that might have exciting and valuable uses in science and in society. It also could be used to build a bomb. For physicists in Europe and the United States, this knowledge brought fear because much of the work had been done in Germany, and no one knew how much German science was devoted to the military exploration of atomic fission. In his August 1939 letter to President Franklin D. Roosevelt, Albert Einstein wrote of this fear. He said, "This new phenomenon would also lead to the construction of bombs, and it is conceivable—though much less certain—that extremely powerful bombs of a new type may thus be constructed. A single bomb of this type, carried by boat and exploded in a port, might very well destroy the whole port together with some of the surrounding territory." Einstein added a warning that Germany had stopped selling any uranium from its mining operations, and he feared that this action showed that the government was seriously interested in the uranium fission experiments at the Kaiser Wilhelm Institute. The Nazis, Einstein worried, could already be stockpiling uranium to experiment with building an atomic bomb.

Quoted in *American Experience,* "Primary Resources: Letter from Albert Einstein to FDR, 8/2/39," PBS. www.pbs.org.

innocent of persecuting others. She also sent food packages to scientists and their families who were suffering hardships in occupied Germany. Although her friendship with Hahn was permanently injured, she continued to treat him well until he died in July 1968, just three months before her own death. She never publicly complained about his denial of her role in the fission discovery. She always declared that he had deserved to win the Nobel Prize.

Later Years

Meitner became a Swedish citizen in 1949. She continued her nuclear research with an emphasis on the peacetime use of atomic energy and lived a comfortable life. She retired in 1954 at the age of seventy-five. Then, in 1960, she moved to England, where Frisch had relocated, to be close to him and his family. She was eighty-two years old.

Hahn never acknowledged Meitner's part in the discovery of nuclear fission, but the physics community outside of Germany did. In 1966 the US Atomic Energy Commission awarded its Enrico Fermi Prize jointly to Meitner, Hahn, and Strassman for their work on fission. It was one of many awards and honors given to Meitner in her later years. In 1997, years after her death, the physics world announced one more honor: a newly discovered element would be formally named for her. Element 109 is known to science as meitnerium (Mt).

Meitner died on October 27, 1968, just a few days before her ninetieth birthday. Frisch placed the following inscription on her gravestone: "Lise Meitner: a physicist who never lost her humanity."[9]

CHAPTER 2

Pearl Kendrick

When Pearl Kendrick was three years old, she came down with whooping cough, or pertussis, as it is scientifically known. Fortunately she recovered, and as medical writer Tim Anderson says, "Four and one-half decades later she would have her revenge, developing the first effective vaccine to combat the ravenous disease."[10] Born on August 24, 1890, in Wheaton, Illinois, Pearl was the daughter of a minister. Her family later moved to Sherburne, New York, where Pearl attended high school. She graduated from high school in 1908 and then received a degree in zoology from Syracuse University in 1914, with a minor in philosophy. During that time, reports historian Carolyn G. Shapiro-Shapin, her teachers said she was "a first class student, thorough, accurate and rapid."[11]

After college Kendrick began her career as a high school science teacher and worked as a high school principal, but her true interest was in public health. While she was working she continued her education by taking graduate school classes at Columbia University, concentrating on the new specialty of bacteriology. Identification of bacteria, the role that bacteria play in infectious diseases, and how to protect people against these germs with vaccines and public health measures were topics that were advancing medical science at a rapid rate. Kendrick was fascinated by the promise for the future.

A Public Health Career

In 1919 Kendrick decided to leave the field of education and accepted a position as a laboratory assistant with the New York State Department of Health. During that time public health departments in the United States were routinely analyzing water and milk to ensure public safety from bacterial disease. In New York, public health laboratories were also researching other ways to prevent diseases. Kendrick soon proved herself to be a competent and skilled researcher, and a little more than a year later, she was offered a better position in Lansing, Michigan. C.C. Young, the director of the Michigan Department of Health's Bureau of Laboratories, asked her to join his growing team. He told her, "I am sure that we can make it interesting for you and there is every chance for advancement."[12] Kendrick accepted the invitation, and her laboratory work was so good that when the Michigan Department of Health opened a West Michigan branch in Grand Rapids in 1926, she was put in charge of the division. She dedicated herself to the Michigan Department of Health's goals of reducing the death rate of Michigan's citizens through public education, infectious disease research, and the distribution of free vaccines to the population. At the same time, Young encouraged Kendrick to take regular leaves of absence to continue her education. She was awarded a doctorate in bacteriology from Johns Hopkins University in 1932.

The Scourge of Whooping Cough

In that same year a virulent epidemic of whooping cough broke out among the children of Grand Rapids. During the 1920s scientists had developed several vaccines to protect against dangerous diseases, including typhoid, smallpox, diphtheria, and tetanus, but no one had yet found an effective protection against whooping cough. *Bordetella pertussis,* the bacterium that causes

Pearl Kendrick worked tirelessly to develop a vaccine against whooping cough; her eventual success resulted in a dramatic drop in deaths from the disease.

whooping cough, was identified in 1906; however, the disease had proved resistant to treatments and vaccines. In the United States alone, more than six thousand children died of the respiratory disease every year. The younger the child, the more likely he or she was to die after contracting whooping cough. In essence, many children coughed themselves to death, breaking blood vessels in their brains and suffering lung damage and seizures. Children endured long bouts of choked coughing from the thick mucus in their respiratory tracts. The coughing spells were so extreme that the children often turned beet red and vomited. As the victims gasped to draw breath after a coughing bout, they made the sucking, whooping sound that gives pertussis its common name. It was a fearsome disease that killed more infants than measles, tuberculosis, polio, scarlet fever, and diphtheria.

All that medicine or science had to offer during an epidemic was to teach parents how to avoid contagion from other children. Public health departments relied on quarantines to protect communities from the spread of whooping cough. In Grand Rapids, for example, children with whooping cough and any siblings (healthy or ill) were required to remain isolated at home for a period of four weeks. They could return to school only if they had a doctor's note certifying them free of the disease. In Chicago, the required isolation period was only two weeks, but for the next three weeks the child could walk outside on public streets only with an attendant and only if wearing a yellow armband marked *whooping cough* in big black letters. In most cities, placards were placed on the doors of homes where whooping cough was identified, warning others to stay away. Around the country, parents and public health officials lived in fear whenever an outbreak occurred in the community.

To Fight a Deadly Disease

In 1932 this was the situation Kendrick faced as whooping cough attacked the children of Grand Rapids. She decided to tackle developing a pertussis vaccine, and toward that end she hired another woman, Grace Eldering, to assist her in the Grand Rapids laboratory. Eldering had been working as an unpaid volunteer at the Lansing laboratory. She had been a teacher but had returned to college to study bacteriology and had a strong interest in public health. She had also survived whooping cough at the age of five and never forgot how awful the experience was. She was an eager partner in Kendrick's proposed project.

It was the height of the Great Depression, however, and no funds were available for Kendrick and Eldering to begin a pertussis study. Nevertheless, Kendrick wrote to Young and asked permission to start a community research project. His reply was tolerant if a little condescending. He answered, "If you are having any fun working on whooping cough, go ahead."[13] Basically, Young's permission meant that Kendrick and Eldering could pursue their whooping cough research only after all of the lab's regular daily work was done, but they were still enthusiastic.

> **"If you are having any fun working on whooping cough, go ahead."[13]**
>
> *—Michigan Health Department director C.C. Young, when asked for permission to perform whooping cough research.*

In lieu of funding, the two worked to form partnerships in the community, enlisting the voluntary cooperation of doctors, public health nurses, and parents in their project. The first job was to collect samples of *Bordetella pertussis* bacteria from sick children and figure out a way to grow the samples on petri dishes in the lab so that the bacteria could be studied. When local doctors reported a case of whooping cough, the women visited the home (with the parents' permission) and collected a sample of the infecting germs by having the child cough onto a cough plate (a small dish of nutrient gel). Then they took the plates back to the lab in order to grow the bacteria on the plates. Public health nurses and private nurses helped by collecting cough-plate samples, too, and bringing them to the lab. Despite the community's help, the women worked long hours in sad conditions to collect their samples. Eldering remembered,

> We learned about the disease and the Depression at the same time. Many of the families were very poor and their living conditions pitiful. . . . We collected specimens by the light of kerosene lamps, from whooping, vomiting, strangling children. We saw what the disease could do. In the laboratory we isolated the pertussis bacillus, not from every patient, but from most of them in the early stages of the disease. . . . The cultures were saved and studied in every possible way.[14]

First Successes

Kendrick and Eldering developed an improved growth medium, or nutrient gel, that allowed them to grow large colonies of *Bordetella pertussis* rapidly and to compare the number of bacteria taken from children at different stages of the disease. This innovation allowed them to use the plates as a diagnostic tool. The bacteria grew so fast that doctors could use the plates to accurately diagnose whooping cough within forty-eight hours. In a 1934 research article for the *American Journal of Public Health,* Kendrick and Eldering explained, "The laboratory findings are being used by the City Health Department in obtaining earlier diagnosis of pertussis and thereby, it is hoped, more effective isolation of cases in their most infective stage."[15] This was an important advance in controlling the spread of whooping cough.

The two women also learned to determine, for the first time, how long an infected child was contagious to others. Kendrick and Eldering discovered that in the first three weeks of the illness, coughs produced active bacteria. By the fourth week,

Easier for the Children

During the early 1940s Pearl Kendrick began to consider the multiple vaccinations then available to and recommended for children. She knew children often dreaded the shots and thought that the number of injections might be reduced. She and Eldering began to work on a way to combine the pertussis vaccines with diphtheria vaccines. In explaining their effort, Kendrick said to a news reporter, "It seemed possible to combine [the vaccines] to save the poor children all that discomfort." The women discovered that combining both vaccines actually increased the effectiveness of the diphtheria vaccine. The pertussis vaccine acted as an adjuvant—a facilitator of the immune response—for diphtheria vaccines. The tetanus vaccine also seemed to enhance the effectiveness of both of the other vaccines, and soon all three vaccines were combined and given together. Thus, the DPT shot—a variation of which is still used today—was created.

Quoted in Virginia Law Burns, *Bold Women in Michigan History.* Missoula, MT: Mountain Press, 2006, p. 76.

most coughs were clear of bacteria, and by the fifth week, 90 percent of children were no longer contagious. Now good quarantine lengths could be established. The Grand Rapids Health Department set a recommended quarantine period of thirty-five days.

A Lifesaving Vaccine

Their ability to grow the pertussis bacteria rapidly and reliably made it possible for Kendrick and Eldering to begin their vaccine research project in earnest in 1933. For the most part they worked after hours, learning to kill, or deactivate, the cultures with cold temperatures and a chemical called thimerosal. They sterilized and purified the resultant vaccine and injected it into laboratory animals to test its safety and efficacy. When injected, the vaccine activated the body's immune system even though the bacteria were all dead and harmless. Recognized as foreign invaders, the bacteria caused antibodies to form that signaled the immune system to attack pertussis bacteria. Once formed, those antibodies remained in the body, ready to immediately attack any live pertussis bacteria that invaded, thus providing immunity in cases of future exposure. To be sure that the vaccine was safe for humans, Kendrick and Eldering also injected themselves. The progress toward the development of a successful vaccine was exhilarating. Kendrick later remembered, "When the work day was over, we started on the research because it was fun. We'd come home, feed the dogs, get some dinner and get back to what was interesting."[16]

> "When the work day was over, we started on the research because it was fun. We'd come home, feed the dogs, get some dinner and get back to what was interesting."[16]
>
> *—Pearl Kendrick*

The dedication paid off. By 1934 the vaccine was ready to be tested among the children of Grand Rapids. The whole community cooperated and participated. Between 1934 and 1936, about 1,600 children were enrolled in a vaccine trial, with 712

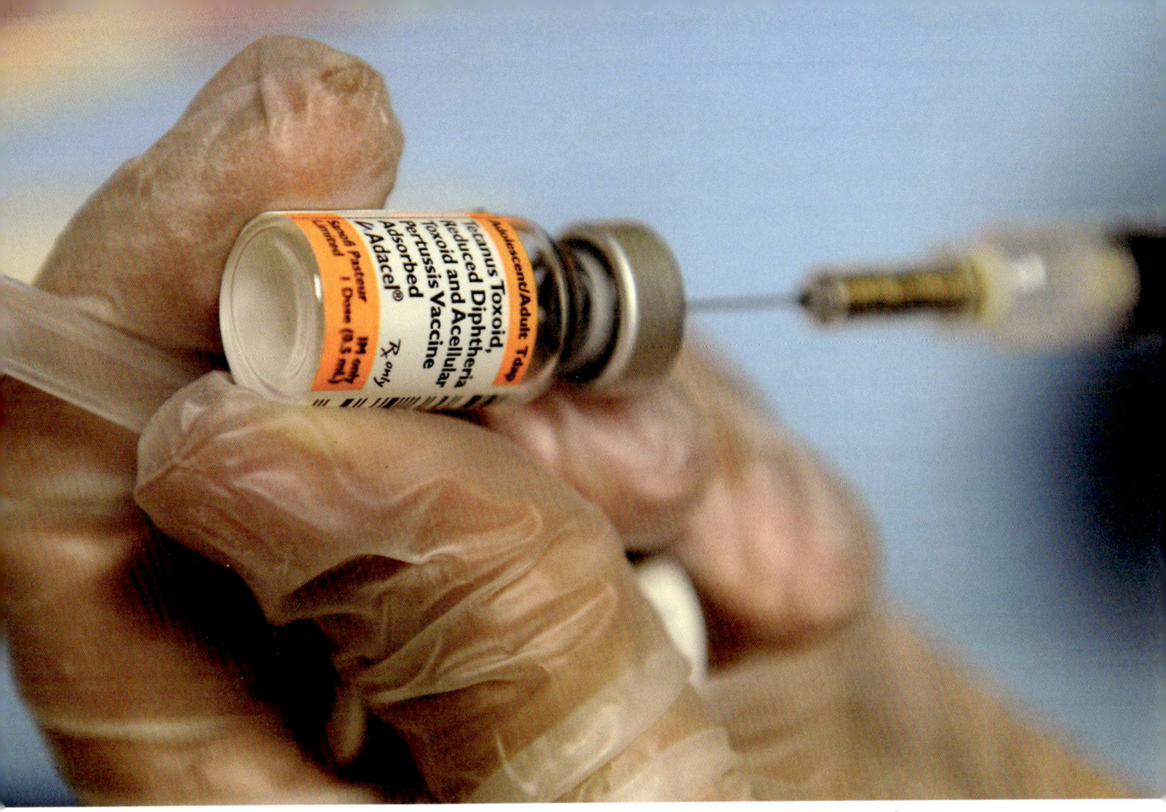

A nurse draws Tdap (tetanus, diphtheria, and pertussis) serum into a syringe. Pearl Kendrick and her coworker, Grace Eldering, discovered that combining the vaccines increased their effectiveness against these three diseases.

receiving the new vaccine and 880 control subjects who were not vaccinated. At the end of the study, only four of the vaccinated children had contracted whooping cough, all mild cases. Forty-five of the unvaccinated group had caught the disease. The results were extremely encouraging, but the number of test subjects was a bit too small to be real proof that the vaccine was effective.

First Lady Eleanor Roosevelt helped Kendrick to get more funding to hire people to produce larger quantities of the vaccine and perform a larger trial. Young, now enthusiastic about the project, allotted a portion of his lab's federal funds to the study also. The new vaccine trial in 1939 included more than 4,000 children, as eager parents sought to get their children into the study and protect them from whooping cough. The successful results were so dramatic that by 1940 both the entire state of Michigan and most states across the country

An Immeasurable Contribution

After Pearl Kendrick died, Richard Remington, dean of the School of Public Health at the University of Michigan, wrote of her legacy,

> **A life saved by prevention cannot even be identified. Who are the men and women living today who would be dead from whooping cough had it not been for Pearl Kendrick's vaccine? We can conclude with reasonable certainty that several hundred thousand of them are now leading productive lives, in this country alone. But who are they? Name one. You can't do it and neither can I. . . . The accomplishments of disease prevention are statistical and epidemiological. Where's the news value, the human interest in that? . . . But a public service orientation can provide more than ample compensation. Dr. Kendrick never became rich and, outside a relatively small circle of informed friends and colleagues, never became famous. All she did was save hundreds of thousands of lives at modest cost. Secure knowledge of that fact is the very best reward.**

Quoted in Carolyn G. Shapiro-Shapin, "Pearl Kendrick, Grace Eldering, and the Pertussis Vaccine," *Emerging Infectious Diseases,* vol. 16, no. 8, August 2010. www.ncbi.nlm.nih.gov/pmc/articles/PMC3298325/.

were producing and distributing the vaccine to America's children. Cases of whooping cough and whooping cough deaths dropped drastically. In Michigan, for example, between 1932 and 1936, 732 children had died of the disease. By 1948, that number was fewer than 30.

For the Good of the World

Kendrick and Eldering were acclaimed nationally and internationally for their defeat of a killer disease. Kendrick traveled to several countries, including Great Britain and Mexico, to help them establish vaccine programs. She shared her research findings, bacterial cultures, and vaccines with scientists around the world. She acted as a consultant for the World Health Organization to assist in vaccination efforts in poor countries. In 1951 Kendrick retired from the Michigan Department of Health and accepted a position as an assistant professor at the University of Michigan's School of Public Health, lecturing and doing research in epidemiology (the medical science of the incidence and control of diseases in populations). Eldering, who had earned her doctorate from Johns Hopkins University in 1942, took over as the director of the Grand Rapids laboratory.

Both women remained modest and humble about their accomplishments. Kendrick was a very private, unassuming person who avoided publicity whenever possible and never sought recognition for her success. She officially retired in 1960 but kept up her work at the University of Michigan as a professor emerita. In 1971, at the age of eighty, she continued to insist that the development of the whooping cough vaccine should be credited not to her but to the whole Grand Rapids community. She told a reporter, "There were so many persons involved, don't make me out as the only one."[17] Pearl Kendrick died of breast cancer on October 8, 1980, at the age of ninety.

CHAPTER 3

Virginia Apgar

Virginia Apgar was born in Westfield, New Jersey, on June 7, 1909. She was the younger of the two surviving children of Charles and Helen Apgar. Charles was an insurance executive with strong science interests, including astronomy, electricity, and radio waves. The whole family loved music, and Virginia played the violin. She also absorbed her father's love of science while still quite young. Everyone in the family was full of energy and curiosity and enjoyed involvement in multiple activities. As an adult Virginia described her family as "people who never sat down."[18] She was the same way throughout her life. By the time she was in high school, she already had made the decision to become a medical doctor. She was an excellent student, and her friends described her as having amazing energy.

Apgar graduated from high school and entered Mount Holyoke College in 1925. There, too, her unbounded energy impressed friends and teachers alike. She depended on scholarships and various part-time jobs throughout college. (One of those jobs was catching feral cats for the school's biology laboratories.) She played seven different sports, acted in college drama productions, was a reporter for the school newspaper, and played violin in college orchestra concerts. At the same time, she was majoring in zoology and remained an excellent student. One of her professors, Christianna Smith, wrote in a scholarship recommendation for Apgar, "It is seldom that one finds a student so thoroughly immersed in her subject and with such a wide knowledge of it."[19]

Establishing a Career

Apgar graduated from college in 1929 and entered medical school at the Columbia College of Physicians and Surgeons. She was one of only three women in the class and graduated with honors in 1933. Then she got a surgical internship at Presbyterian Hospital (now known as New York–Presbyterian/Columbia University Medical Center). Apgar loved surgery and was highly skilled, but the specialty was a difficult choice for a woman at the time. Her chief of surgery, Alan Whipple, suggested that she switch specialties. He worried that a woman surgeon would have a hard time making a living. Apgar knew that Whipple's advice was sound. She later commented, "Even women won't go to a woman surgeon."[20] So, after two years in surgery, Apgar took Whipple's advice and entered the new medical specialty of anesthesiology.

> "Even women won't go to a woman surgeon."[20]
>
> —*Virginia Apgar*

Anesthesiology was just becoming a medical discipline during the 1930s. Traditionally doctors had paid little attention to anesthesia. The surgeons left that to nurses and did not consider knowledge of anesthesia particularly important. Apgar had to receive her training first from nurses at Presbyterian and then at the University of Wisconsin—the only medical school offering training in anesthesiology at the time. In 1938, at the age of twenty-nine, she became the first director of the new anesthesiology division at Presbyterian Hospital. She not only worked as an anesthesiologist, but she also recruited young doctors to the specialty, set up a formal residency program, and developed medical school training courses. She persuaded surgeons to accept anesthesiologists as equals and helped to raise the status and prestige of anesthesiologists throughout the country. By the 1940s surgeons were accepting anesthesiologists as critically important members of operating room teams.

Despite Apgar's achievements in advancing the field of anesthesiology and in developing Presbyterian Hospital's Anesthesiology Department, in 1949 hospital administrators passed her over to name a man as head of the department. Apgar was named a full professor at the medical school instead, but it was not enough to fulfill her. She also joined the staff at Sloane Hospital, the obstetrics and gynecology service within Presbyterian Hospital, working in the delivery room as an anesthesiologist. Author and doctor Marion Hunt says of this decision, "In this position, which combined the strands of her experience, training, and research interests, Apgar would make the discoveries that were to shape the development of neonatal medicine."[21]

Who Will Care for the Babies?

Neonates are infants under four weeks old, but in 1950 there was no medical neonatal specialty—neonatology. Newborns in the delivery room were generally ignored by doctors, who concentrated on the mother. Fetal monitors—to check a baby's status before and during delivery—had not yet been invented. Pediatricians saw children after birth and once they were at home, but none of them, as Columbia pediatrician Emmet Holt says, believed that neonatal medicine was a "real field."[22] As a result, newborns with trouble breathing or whose hearts were not beating effectively or who had other difficulties often died in the delivery room or soon thereafter. In the United States, in general, maternal mortality rates had dropped significantly between 1930 and 1950, as more deliveries were performed in hospitals. Infant and childhood mortality rates were also much improved because of improved medical care. However, newborn mortality rates remained the same in 1950 as they had been in 1930. The US mortality statistic was about fifty-eight neonatal deaths for every one thousand births. Many obstetricians truly believed that little could

Virginia Apgar is considered to have founded the field of neonatology—the medical care of infants less than four weeks old.

be done for a neonate in trouble and that the newborn should be allowed to die naturally. Modern medical doctor Alan Fleischman explains that "it was considered better not to be aggressive. You dried them, you shook them, and some doctors patted them on the backside and that was it."[23]

In the delivery room, Apgar quickly became troubled by this neglect. She thought that many of these babies could be saved and began to think about what could be done to improve their health and survival. Using her acute observational skills, she noticed how newborns' distress was correlated with factors such as delivery complications, prematurity, and anesthesia given to

A-P-G-A-R

In 1961 Dr. Joseph Butterfield of Denver, Colorado, wrote to Virginia Apgar that one of his residents had come up with a mnemonic using her name to help him remember her five scoring criteria for newborns. Apgar was pleased with the mnemonic, and it was soon adopted everywhere. It looks like this, with each letter of her last name standing for a criterion:

A—Appearance (color)

P—Pulse (heart rate)

G—Grimace (reflex irritability)

A—Activity (muscle tone)

R—Respiration

Today the mnemonic is so connected with the scoring system that many people do not know that the letters actually represent the name of the developer of the system.

the mother. She saw simple methods of distinguishing between a normal, strong neonate and one who needed medical intervention. The newborn with feeble breathing, a blue color to its skin (indicating lack of oxygen), or a weak or absent cry might live if given immediate help. The obstetrician, however, was busy with the mother, and pediatricians were not even present in the delivery room. So the anesthesiologist was the logical person to help the baby. Apgar began using the newborn's signs of distress to decide to intervene. She cleared the baby's airway and administered oxygen or performed mouth-to-mouth resuscitation. Infant mortality dropped, and Apgar began teaching her students to employ the same methods in the delivery room.

The Apgar Scoring System

One day a medical student approached Apgar in the cafeteria and asked her how doctors could assess a neonate's status and whether it needed resuscitation. Hardly stopping to think, Apgar replied, "That's easy, you would do it like this."[24] She grabbed a nearby piece of paper and jotted down five categories to observe:

heart rate, respiration, muscle tone, color, and reflexes. Apgar stared at what she had written, thought about the implications, and rushed out of the room to begin testing her system immediately. By 1952 she had used her idea to develop a scoring system to observe and assess more than one thousand infants at one minute after birth. The scoring of her test was simple: In each of the five categories, an infant was given a score of 0, 1, or 2. For example, a neonate not breathing received a 0; one whose breathing was difficult or weak received a 1; and a baby who breathed strongly received a 2. In each category, 0 was a poor score, 1 was a weak score, and 2 was a healthy score. In 1952 Apgar described her scoring system at a professional meeting and then published it in 1953. It looks like this:

	0	1	2
Heart Rate	Absent	< 100 per minute	100–140 per minute
Respiration	Absent	Irregular	Strong, crying
Reflex Irritability	Absent	Weak	Grimace, sneeze
Muscle Tone	Flaccid	Some flexion	Strong flexion
Color	Blue	Extremities blue	Pink[25]

Altogether, a newborn can receive a total score between 0 and 10. The lower the score, the more obvious it is that the neonate requires help. A score lower than 7 means that resuscitation efforts should be used.

The medical community at large quickly accepted Apgar's scoring system, and it changed the way that neonates were cared for throughout the country and then the world. It became the standard to score the neonate at one minute and again at five minutes in order to determine how well resuscitation efforts had worked. Writing for the March of Dimes (a nonprofit organization dedicated to the health of mothers and babies), David Rose says, "In essence, the Apgar score was revolutionary because it was the first clinical method to recognize the newborn's needs as a patient. It helped spur the development of neonatology as a

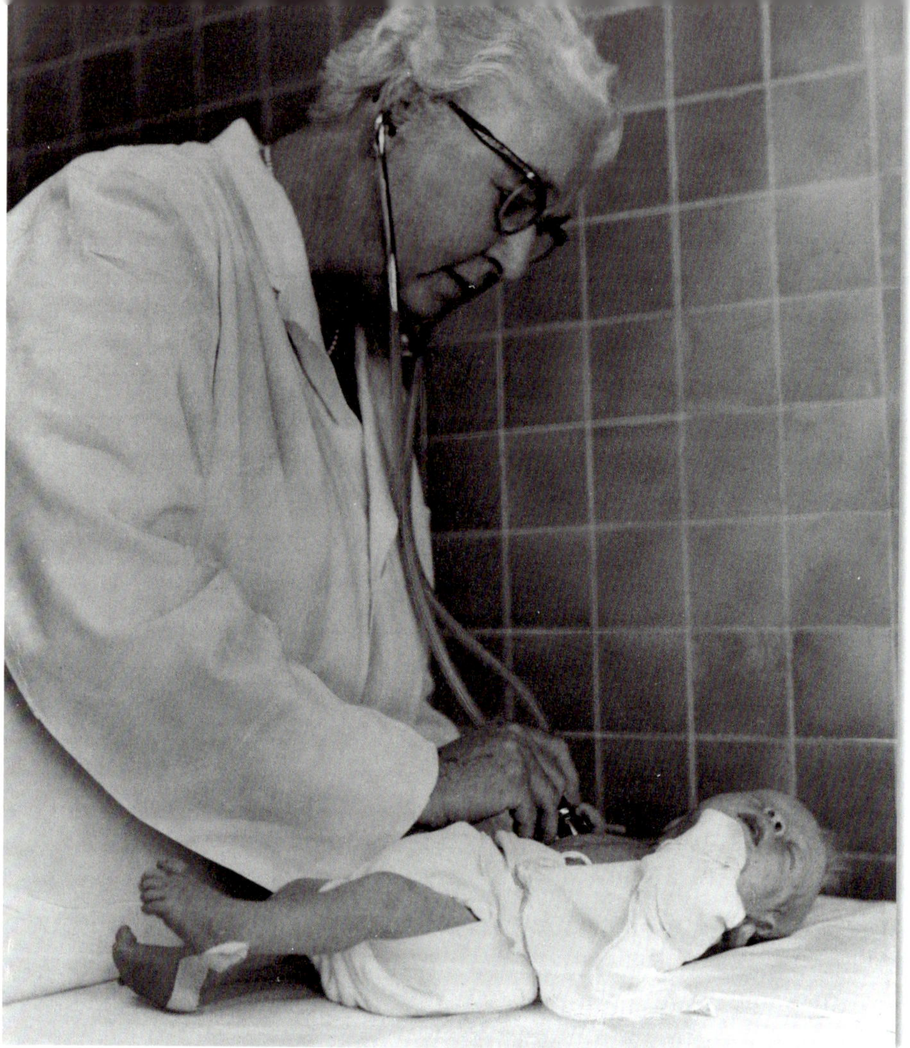

Virginia Apgar uses a stethoscope to assess the health of a newborn infant. Apgar not only taught her students how to spot signs that a newborn needed immediate help but also researched techniques to improve neonatal health.

medical focus, establishing the need for protocols and facilities such as the newborn intensive care unit to provide specialized care."[26]

Acting to Save Infant Lives

Apgar continued her research of newborn mortality for the next seven years. She wanted to determine precisely the factors that underlay low Apgar scores. She assembled a team of doctors to study how labor, delivery, and anesthesia affected a newborn baby's condition. While studying more than fifteen thousand babies, the team developed new ways to measure an infant's blood gases (such as the oxygen and carbon dioxide) as well as the amount of anesthesia in the blood. At that time, many women in labor and most women undergoing cesarean births were given a general anesthesia called cyclopropane. The research team discovered that cyclopropane was easily passed to the baby from the mother's body and that the infants were anesthetized too. Their blood gases were badly affected, and the newborns had low Apgar scores. The anesthesia was putting neonates at risk and causing a need for resuscitation. Using the term *gas* to refer to anesthesia, Apgar immediately said, "There goes my favorite gas."[27] She never used it in the delivery room again, and she quickly persuaded the world that general anesthesia given to a mother could threaten her baby's life. Apgar pioneered the use of local anesthesia—numbing only the body parts affected by labor and delivery—during the birthing process.

> "In essence, the Apgar score was revolutionary because it was the first clinical method to recognize the newborn's needs as a patient."[26]
>
> *—David Rose of the March of Dimes.*

The team's research also revealed that infants born in the wrong position (feet first, or breech birth), by cesarean section, or aided in delivery by the use of forceps were at risk and often needed quick assessment and attention in order to survive. Apgar warned all anesthesiologists and medical personnel caring for newborns, "Time is of the utmost importance. Delay is damaging to the infant. Act promptly, accurately, and gently."[28] As the culture of the medical community changed, neonatal mortality dropped drastically. From 1952 until today, there has been a 75 percent drop in infant deaths, thanks in large part to Virginia Apgar.

A New Career with the March of Dimes

In 1958 Apgar took a leave of absence from Columbia to get a master's degree in public health at Johns Hopkins University. She wanted to improve her statistical research abilities, and she was

Ready for Action

Apgar specialized in resuscitating neonates, but she was devoted to the idea that people in respiratory trouble—regardless of age—could be saved with quick thinking and quick action. She often declared, "Nobody, but nobody, is going to stop breathing on me." Even when she was out and about, walking down the street or riding public transportation or in any public place, she was ready to react in an emergency. She made it her habit to always carry a penknife, bandages, and a small airway tube on her person wherever she went. That way, if she saw a person having trouble breathing, she could jump into action, establish an airway, and save a life. She once claimed that during her lifetime she had used her airway tube at sixteen different auto accident sites to resuscitate victims.

Quoted in Melinda Beck, "How's Your Baby? Recalling the Apgar Score's Namesake," *Wall Street Journal,* May 26, 2009. www.wsj.com.

becoming more and more interested in birth defects and how to prevent them. In 1959 she accepted a position to lead the Division of Congenital Malformations with the National Foundation of the March of Dimes. She remained with the foundation for fifteen years, eventually becoming the vice president for medical affairs and working tirelessly for its mission of preventing birth defects. David Rose writes of her efforts,

> Dr. Apgar could be hailed as the "founder" of our interest in prematurity, for it was she who first brought attention to the problems of premature birth, as early as 1960. . . . In her March of Dimes career she orchestrated a campaign for immunization against rubella [German measles], promoted the establishment of birth defects registries, and insisted that genetic history and pregnancy history be made a routine part of medical record-keeping for pregnant women.[29]

A Universal Practice

Apgar died of liver disease on August 7, 1974, at the age of sixty-five, but she never retired and remained energetic and active until shortly before her death. In 1972 she cowrote with journalist Joan Beck the popular book *Is My Baby All Right?* The book explains some of the causes of birth defects and describes the best ways to have a healthy pregnancy and a healthy baby. It was Apgar who came up with the March of Dimes slogan "Be good to your baby before it's born."[30] In the last year of her life, she traveled to three continents, covering 83,000 miles (133,576 km) in order to teach and publicize the importance of fighting birth defects.

> **"Time is of the utmost importance. Delay is damaging to the infant. Act promptly, accurately, and gently."[28]**
>
> —*Virginia Apgar*

Today it is a universal practice to assign every newborn an Apgar score at one and five minutes after birth. The National Library of Medicine says of her legacy, "It has been said that every baby born in a modern hospital anywhere in the world is looked at first through the eyes of Dr. Virginia Apgar."[31]

CHAPTER 4

Jane Goodall

Born on April 3, 1934, in London, England, Valerie Jane Goodall grew up loving animals and nature. For her first birthday her father gave her a stuffed chimpanzee that she named Jubilee; it was her favorite toy for years. As a toddler she once tried to bring several earthworms to bed with her; her mother did not scold her but just carried the worms back outside. When Valerie Jane was five years old, she terrified her family by disappearing. Sure she was lost, they called the police, and family, neighbors, and police searched for the little girl until dark. At that point a disheveled child appeared, to everyone's great relief. "Wherever have you been?"[32] asked her mother. Valerie Jane explained that she had wanted to know how a chicken could lay an egg and where it came from. She hid under a pile of straw in the henhouse, lay perfectly still, and watched a hen on her nest for five hours until finally the hen laid her egg, and the child's desire to understand was satisfied. Again, her mother did not scold her but listened to her daughter's excited story. As an adult, Goodall reflected on this memory: "Looking back, it is the making of a little scientist: curiosity and questions, not getting the right answer, trying to find out for yourself, making a mistake, not giving up, trying another way and learning patience."[33]

Becoming Jane

As Valerie Jane grew older, her favorite books were the stories of Dr. Doolittle and Tarzan. She began to dream of going to Africa and living with the animals. Throughout her childhood, she lived in the country, with her mother and maternal grandmother. Valerie Jane's father was absent most of the time. He was away in the military during the years of World War II and later became estranged from Goodall's mother. Nevertheless, Valerie Jane had a happy childhood in her country home. She established a nature club with her friends, went on nature walks, and enjoyed a variety of pets. She collected bird nests, caterpillars (which she kept healthy and well fed), and plant leaves, seeds, and buds. She had dogs, turtles, chickens, and guinea pigs, and she carefully observed the lives of all the birds that lived in her backyard. When she was older and went away to school, she rode horses as well.

As Goodall's school years came to an end, she began to think about the future and what she would do with her life. Also around this time, her parents finally divorced, and she decided that she did not like the name *Valerie*. She started calling herself simply *Jane*. Jane daydreamed about going to Africa to study and write about animals, but her family did not even have the money to allow her to go to college, despite her good grades at school. Her mother suggested secretarial school because people always need secretaries anywhere in the world. Perhaps as a secretary she could travel to Africa someday. In 1953 Goodall moved to London and entered a one-year course at secretarial school.

The Chance of a Lifetime

Goodall was a good secretary, but she was bored. Then, in May 1956, an old school friend whose father had just bought a farm in Kenya wrote and invited Goodall to come for a visit. Goodall accepted the invitation immediately. She quit her job and returned home to live in order to save money on rent and living expenses. She took a job nearby as a waitress, and began saving every penny to pay for the trip to Kenya. By the spring of 1957 she was on her way, and after a three-week ocean voyage, she finally arrived in Africa. She wrote home, "I really do simply adore Kenya. It is so wild, uncultivated, primitive, mad, exciting, unpredictable. . . . I am living in the Africa I have always longed for, always felt stirring in my blood."[34]

Goodall spent about twenty months living and working in Kenya, and during that time she had the good fortune to meet the famous and influential anthropologist and paleontologist Louis Leakey. Leakey was studying fossils and exploring the origins of humans in Africa. Goodall impressed Leakey as she told him about her love for animals and her desire to work in Africa. Leakey asked her whether she would be interested in conducting field studies of some chimpanzees living in a game preserve in Tanganyika (now Tanzania) if he could arrange financing for the project. Goodall leaped at the chance, but she had to return home for a year while Leakey worked on getting government permission and funding. The money came through, but there was a big problem for Tanganyika's officials. They would not allow a young woman to go into the wilds alone. It was too dangerous. Goodall's mother volunteered to go with her as a companion; Tanganyika agreed, and so, in the summer of 1960, at the age of twenty-six, Goodall finally arrived at the Gombe Stream Chimpanzee Reserve on the shore of Lake Tanganyika to begin her life's work.

> "I am living in the Africa I have always longed for, always felt stirring in my blood."[34]
>
> —*Jane Goodall*

Gombe and the Chimpanzees

The conditions in the camp at Gombe Stream were primitive. The women lived in tents, and it was cold at night and stiflingly hot by day. Both women came down with a malarial fever that lasted a month. In addition, supplies could be brought in only by boat, and they were alone except for a local cook who came with them and a few people who visited sometimes from a nearby village. But Goodall was where she wanted to be. She had no

Jane Goodall and her husband, wildlife photographer Hugo van Lawick, prepare a camera as one of their subjects investigates.

experience, training, or higher education, but she had unlimited patience, observational skills, determination, and a passion for studying the chimpanzees. Armed with binoculars and a notepad and pen for taking field notes, she was ready to learn about chimp behavior in the wild—something no one had ever accomplished before. She later said, "I remember my first day, looking up from the shore to the forest, hearing the apes and the birds, and smelling the plants, and thinking this is very, very unreal. Then I started walking through the forest and as soon as a chimp saw me, it would run away."[35]

Breaking the Rules

Since she was not formally trained as a scientist when she began her study of chimpanzees, Jane Goodall broke a lot of formal observational rules. Scientists insisted that observers had to be objective, and that meant no emotional attachments or human labeling of behavior or animals. Animal observers assigned their subjects specific numbers. Goodall never thought of such a thing. She knew right away that the chimps she studied were true individuals who had much in common with people. She gave her chimps names. They were David Greybeard, Fifi, Frodo, Flint, and Goliath, and all were unique characters to her. She always refused to change that approach. She once said, "These people were trying to make ethology [the study of animal behavior] a hard science. So they objected—quite unpleasantly—to me naming my subjects and for suggesting that they had personalities, minds and feelings. I didn't care." In the end, Goodall's position won out. Today many ethologists name their subjects, and no one questions the practice.

Quoted in Robin McKie, "Chimps with Everything: Jane Goodall's 50 Years in the Jungle," *Guardian,* June 26, 2010. www.theguardian.com.

For weeks the chimpanzees ran away whenever Goodall tried to get close enough to make observations, but with great carefulness and sensitivity, she finally was able to overcome their fear and gain their trust. This was Goodall's first major contribution to science. She demonstrated that wild animals could be habituated to a human presence and that their natural behavior could be studied in their natural habitat. In that first year Goodall made three other momentous discoveries about chimpanzees: She saw chimpanzees eating meat, although at the time all scientists believed that chimps were vegetarians. In a sudden rainstorm, she watched a group of chimpanzees perform a display or dance, which she labeled a "Rain Festival";[36] it was evidence that chimps have a culture. And she saw chimpanzees making and using tools—twigs stripped of leaves, fashioned to fish termites from their mounds. This last discovery amazed scientists, who had always said that only humans make tools. When Leakey heard of this behavior, he said, "Now we must redefine 'tool,' redefine 'man,' or accept chimpanzees as humans."[37]

A World-Renowned Expert

Goodall was deeply pleased with her achievements. She now knew more than any human being on Earth about chimpanzees. On July 14, 1961, she wrote to her family, "The challenge has been met. The hills & forests are my home. And what is more, I think my mind works like a chimp's, subconsciously."[38] Leakey was thrilled by Goodall's success and was able to interest the National Geographic Society in funding her research. The organization sent photographer Hugo van Lawick to document Goodall's work, and when *National Geographic* magazine published beautiful articles and photos of her and Gombe Stream's chimpanzees, Goodall became famous. Leakey also persuaded Cambridge University to accept Goodall into its doctoral program in ethology, even though she did not have a college degree. He had to persuade Goodall to accept the idea, too, but he believed her work would be taken more seriously by other scientists if she had the proper credentials.

By the time Goodall got her doctorate in 1965—while taking many breaks to return to her now beloved chimps at Gombe—she and her chimpanzees were known and loved the world over. In 1964 she and van Lawick married, and in 1967 they had a son, Hugo Eric Louis van Lawick, whom the couple nicknamed "Grub." The primitive Gombe Stream camp became an elaborate permanent encampment with several buildings and groups of researchers and assistants. Grub was raised there, but Goodall and van Lawick divorced when the boy was seven years old. Goodall continued her research into chimp society and made many other discoveries, demonstrating the fascinating complexity of chimpanzees' life and their similarity to humans. She published articles in *National Geographic* and later wrote extremely popular books about her life with the chimpanzees. She had professional standing, became perhaps the most famous and beloved woman scientist in the

> **"Now we must redefine 'tool,' redefine 'man,' or accept chimpanzees as humans."[37]**
>
> *—Louis Leakey, on learning that chimps use tools.*

world, and changed primatology (the study of primates) and scientific observation forever.

The Next Chapter

By 1975 Goodall no longer worked at Gombe full-time. She married Derek Bryceson, the head of the Tanzanian National Park, but he died of cancer in 1980. Goodall then embarked on a second career. She became a conservationist and activist, with the goal of educating humanity about the need to protect the environment, nurture the animals, save chimpanzees, and value all life on the planet. In 1977 Goodall founded the Jane Goodall Institute (JGI) to protect the chimps of Gombe from habitat loss and hunting and to protect all the chimpanzees of Africa from deforestation, poaching, and exploitation. She was also concerned about the African people living in poverty. She encouraged African governments to promote nature tourism that would protect animal habitats while providing jobs for local people.

Learning to Be a Mother

By the time her son was born, Jane Goodall had learned a lot about good mothering from watching chimpanzee behavior. She put some of her knowledge of chimp mother-child interaction to use in her own relationship with her baby. Goodall explains,

> **There are certain characteristics that define a good chimp mother. She is patient, she is protective but she is not over-protective—that is really important. She is tolerant but she can impose discipline. She is affectionate. She plays. And the most important of all: she is supportive. So that if her kid gets into a fight, even if it is with a higher-ranking individual, she will not hesitate to go in and help.**

Goodall decided to be like a good chimp mother with her son, saying, "Do you pick up a crying baby or do you leave it to cry? Let's just say I picked my baby up when he cried."

Quoted in Robin McKie, "Chimps with Everything: Jane Goodall's 50 Years in the Jungle," *Guardian,* June 26, 2010. www.theguardian.com.

Jane Goodall observes a wild chimpanzee. Goodall's care and persistence helped her gain the chimpanzees' trust, allowing her to observe them in their natural habitat.

As time passed, Goodall became passionate about protecting chimps used for scientific research or vivisection and persuading scientists to treat these intelligent animals ethically and move them from laboratories to sanctuaries. She fought for a better life for captive chimpanzees throughout the world and still tries to stop the trade in chimps sold for pets or for entertainment or to zoos. In *Through a Window*, a book she wrote in 1990, she explains,

> The more we learn of the true nature of nonhuman animals, especially those with complex brains and corresponding complex social behaviour, the more ethical concerns are raised regarding their use in the service of man—whether this be in entertainment, as "pets," for food, in research laboratories or any of the other uses to which we subject them. This concern is sharpened when the usage in question leads to intense physical or mental suffering—as is so often true with regard to vivisection.[39]

In 1991 Goodall established Roots & Shoots, a global youth program with thousands of members dedicated to helping the human community, the animal community, and the environment through local community projects. Both the JGI and Roots & Shoots remain successful programs that continue to inspire people worldwide and advocate for the environment and the lives of animals, especially chimpanzees. Her legacy also includes the research of the last fifty years that has been accomplished with animals as diverse as whales, baboons, and ants using her observational methods for studying animals in the wild. In 2003 Goodall was named a dame of the Order of the British Empire by Queen Elizabeth II, one of many honors she has been awarded over her lifetime.

An Abiding Love for Animals

Today, in her eighties, Goodall maintains a home in England and travels the world some three hundred days a year, actively lecturing about the importance of conservation and compassion for animals. She lobbies governments, negotiates with corporations and trade groups, and educates medical research executives about the importance of protecting habitats and animals. She is admired everywhere she goes, and she is still trying to change the world for the better. She has gone from being a quiet, isolated young woman living essentially alone with animals to being a celebrity and an advocate. She says, "It never ceases to amaze me that there's this person who travels around and does all these things. And it's me. It doesn't seem like me at all." Goodall is tireless in her work and knows what an important role she has to play, but she says, "The best days of my life were spent in Gombe's forests."[40]

Jane Goodall learned and taught the world that chimpanzees are individuals, with intelligence and feelings, with social bonds and psychological needs, with dark flaws but also with compassion and sensitivity and, most of all, with value. She has known all her life that humans and chimpanzees are not so very different from one another. She strongly believes that the well-being of all of Earth's creatures is inextricably tied together. She says, "Only if we understand, can we care. Only if we care, we will help. Only if we help, we shall be saved."[41]

CHAPTER 5

Shirley Ann Jackson

When Shirley Ann Jackson was four years old, she told her mother that someday people would call her "Shirley the Great."[42] The very bright, exuberant little girl was born in Washington, DC, on August 5, 1946. Her father was a veteran of World War II and a postal worker and cab driver, and her mother was a social worker. Shirley Ann was the second of their four children, and she grew up in a home that valued education and hard work.

A Remarkably Talented Child

When she was quite young, Shirley Ann showed a talent for science, and her parents encouraged this interest. Her father told her to "aim for the stars so that you reach the treetops and at any rate you'll get off the ground."[43] His advice became her favorite saying. She took to heart the idea of aspiring to anything she chose. In the early 1950s, however, becoming great and aiming high was no easy task. Shirley Ann was an African American child growing up in a segregated area. Even though there was an elementary school close to her home, she had to be driven to the school for black children miles away. The school did not have many resources, but Shirley Ann had the advantage of her home life and parents. Her mother, for instance, taught all the children to read before they went to kindergarten. Then, in 1954, came the US Supreme Court decision known as *Brown v. Board of Education* that ruled segregated schools unconstitutional. Schools were desegregated, and Shirley Ann was relocated to her neighborhood school. She was thrilled by the school's big library and enjoyed the competition with other very bright children.

> **"Aim for the stars so that you reach the treetops and at any rate you'll get off the ground."[43]**
>
> *—Shirley Ann Jackson's father.*

Her teachers quickly recognized Shirley Ann's talent, especially in math and science. When she was ten years old, the little girl was already doing science experiments at home. She collected and studied bumblebees in her backyard, for instance, capturing them in jars, experimenting with their diets, and noting how they responded to sunshine versus darkness or to the presence of a wasp or a yellow jacket. She enjoyed the bees, and she remembers, "I always tried to let them go though, before they died."[44]

Shirley Ann's great love, however, was mathematics—any kind of mathematics. In junior high and high school, she was placed in advanced classes, where she excelled, earning straight As. When she graduated from Roosevelt High School in 1963, she was class valedictorian. The assistant principal told her how extraordinarily talented she was and suggested that she should apply to the Massachusetts Institute of Technology (MIT). Her father was thrilled by the idea, but her mother worried about the prejudice she might face. The young woman knew by that time that she wanted to do something in science and math, and she wanted the best education possible. Jackson remembers, "The idea of going to a place where there were a whole bunch of other smart kids . . . I thought, well, here, I could really do my thing. I wouldn't be a square. I could do all of that. And so that's why it fascinated me. And the more I read about it, the more I became interested in it."[45]

Alone and Determined to Succeed

Jackson entered MIT in 1964, with the plan of studying mathematics and engineering. Then, when she took a physics class as a freshman, she fell in love with the science and knew she had found her niche. But life at MIT was lonely. In a freshman class of nine hundred students, Jackson was one of about forty-five women, and of the four thousand students at MIT, there were fewer than a dozen African Americans. She had to eat by herself in the cafeteria because the white girls would not sit with her. No one would let her join their study groups. She recalls, "I had to work alone. I went through a down period, but at some level you have to decide you will persist in what you're doing and that you won't let people beat you down."[46]

Jackson persisted no matter what kind of prejudice she was facing. One professor said to her that "colored girls should learn a trade," as if he could not believe that she was capable of succeeding at MIT. Jackson was hurt and angry, but she says

Technology for the Environment

In 2013, under Shirley Ann Jackson's leadership, Rensselaer Polytechnic Institute began its Jefferson Project. The project is an interdisciplinary cooperative effort to understand, manage, and protect the ecology of New York's Lake George with cutting-edge technology. The lake is small enough to monitor in detail and isolated enough to be studied as a unique ecology, but it is at risk from environmental threats. Jackson says researchers have made Lake George "the Smartest Lake in the World." They have put up weather stations around the lake. They have sensors in all the lake's tributaries, and other sensors provide data about the lake's bed and measure circulation patterns on its floor. They are studying the chemistry of the lake and its vegetation and animal life. They are keeping track of environmental events to determine what might threaten the health of the lake. Jackson says that ultimately this research will affect "the area of public policy in terms of how this plays into decision-making and the regulations that govern the lake." It is a model that may eventually determine environmental policies throughout the world.

Quoted in Vassar Hub, "5 Questions: RPI President Shirley Ann Jackson," March 31, 2015. http://alums.vassar.edu.

now, “I did choose a trade—I chose physics.”[47] She earned the respect of fellow students and faculty alike with her outstanding academic work. She was so brilliant in her classes that students came to want her in their study groups. She did so well in the class of the professor who told her to learn a trade that he later offered her a job in his laboratory. She graduated with a bachelor of science degree in physics in 1968 and went on to get her doctorate in theoretical elementary particle physics in 1973. She was the first African American woman ever to re-

As chair of the Nuclear Regulatory Commission, Shirley Ann Jackson was in charge of overseeing all the peaceful uses of nuclear energy.

ceive a doctorate at MIT and the second black female to earn a doctorate in physics in the United States. She also contributed to the university in important social ways. She was a leader in forming its first Black Student Union, and she traveled the country to convince bright African American high schoolers to apply to MIT.

The Physics Researcher

Jackson did postdoctoral research at the Fermi National Accelerator Laboratory in Batavia, Illinois, for two years and accepted a position at AT&T Bell Laboratories in New Jersey in 1976. She remained with Bell Labs—first full-time and then as a consultant—until 1995. Jackson was especially interested in subatomic particles (the particles that make up the atoms in everything), and her research in this area was groundbreaking. Jackson studied the movements and actions of very unstable subatomic particles, which are quite short-lived. Her research involved such subatomic particles as bosons, mesons, and neutrinos, and at Bell Labs she was helping to figure out practical applications of the effects of subatomic particles and energy waves in various materials. As mathematics professor Scott Williams explains,

> **"I had to work alone. I went through a down period, but at some level you have to decide you will persist in what you're doing and that you won't let people beat you down."[46]**
>
> *—Shirley Ann Jackson*

> One method [of study] is using a particle accelerator, a device in which nuclei are accelerated to high speeds and then collided with a target to separate them into subatomic particles. Another way of studying them is by detecting their movements using certain kinds of nonconducting solids. When some solids are exposed to high-energy particles, the crystal lattice structure of the atoms is distorted, and this phenomenon leaves marks or tracks that

can be seen with an electron microscope. Photographs of the tracks are then enhanced, and by examining these photographs physicists like Jackson can make predictions about what kinds of particles have caused the marks.[48]

Jackson's particle research contributed to the scientific understanding of the effects of density waves in different materials, especially in semiconductors.

A semiconductor is a material or object that allows some controlled energy (such as electricity or heat) to move through it (or be conducted) and thus can be used in electronic devices. Silicon and germanium are examples of semiconductor materials. Jackson's research into semiconductors and subatomic particles had a direct effect on telecommunications and enabled other researchers to develop such inventions as solar cells, touch-tone telephones, fiber optic cables, and caller ID and call waiting functions on phones.

> "I did choose a trade—I chose physics."[47]
>
> *—Shirley Ann Jackson*

During her years with Bell Labs, Jackson also met her husband, physicist Morris A. Washington. The couple had one son, and when he was young, they took turns alternating working late and caring for the boy. Even though she was continuing her beloved physics and raising a child, Jackson remained interested in public service. She became involved with a Bell Labs program established to encourage and assist young women and African Americans with talent to go to graduate school and get doctorates. She became concerned about furthering higher science education and public policy as it relates to engineering, physics, education, and nuclear power.

Embracing a Public Role

Jackson began to take on public policy and educational issues that related to her skills in physics. In 1985 she was appointed to New Jersey's Commission on Science and Technology. Then

A Quiet Crisis

Shirley Ann Jackson says that there is a "quiet crisis" occurring in the United States that could endanger the future of the country. As she explains,

> The crisis stems from the gap between the nation's growing need for scientists, engineers, and other technically skilled workers, and its production of them. As the generation educated in the 1950s and 1960s prepares to retire, our colleges and universities are not graduating enough scientific and technical talent to step into research laboratories, software and other design centers, refineries, defense installations, science policy offices, manufacturing shop floors and high-tech startups.

Jackson believes that the United States can best solve the problem by encouraging and educating talented people who are often ignored—minorities, women, and people with disabilities. She says, "For the United States to remain competitive in a vibrant global innovation and research environment, it must have access to the best minds. The nation's technological strength depends entirely on its ability to attract, educate, recruit, and retain the best science and engineering workers."

Shirley Ann Jackson, "The Quiet Crisis," Rensselaer Polytechnic Institute. http://rpi.edu.

she served on committees of the National Academy of Sciences, the American Association for the Advancement of Science, and the National Science Foundation. Jackson moved on to serve as an adviser to the US secretary of energy, helping to establish future goals for national energy laboratories, and she joined the Advisory Council of the Institute of Nuclear Power Operations. She was becoming a well-known and highly respected scientist throughout the country, and in 1991 she returned to university life as well. For the next four years Jackson was a physics professor at Rutgers University. She remembers, "I wanted to have graduate students, to build my own research groups."[49] She actively promoted the advancement of women in the sciences, and MIT elected her to lifelong membership on its board of trustees. It was a true honor to Jackson. According to writer Joan Oleck, Jackson "became the ultimate insider at the same institution where once she had been a lonely female minority student on the outside looking in."[50]

In 1995 President Bill Clinton nominated Jackson to be the chairman of the Nuclear Regulatory Commission (NRC). Jackson took on the job of regulating the country's 110 nuclear power plants, overseeing the environmental safeguards, handling the politically touchy subject of nuclear waste, taking care of security issues, and deciding which plants should be allowed to maintain and extend their operating licenses. The NRC oversees all of the peaceful uses of nuclear energy, whether civilian or governmental. Jackson explains,

> The NRC actually does more than oversee nuclear power plants. It's nuclear power reactors. It's research, test, and training reactors, which tend to be at lower power. It oversees fuel-cycle facilities, some aspects of uranium mining, uranium enrichment and fuel fabrication. It oversees the transportation . . . storage and disposal of nuclear wastes, meaning it oversees it in the sense of regulatory oversight. It delegates a lot of the oversight of low-level radioactive wastes to the states, but all of the high-activity, high-level radioactive wastes, including spent nuclear fuel, is directly overseen by the NRC. . . . So it has a broad scope. And imbedded within it as well, it is governed by . . . the various environmental policy acts. So it has the responsibility to protect public health and safety and the environment in the peaceful uses of nuclear energy.[51]

While she was chairman of the NRC, Jackson set in place regulations based on scientific risk assessments and a policy for reviewing and relicensing power plants that is still in use today. She was also instrumental in forming the International Nuclear Regulators Association for the regulation and safety of

As president of Rensselaer Polytechnic Institute, Shirley Ann Jackson presides over commencement exercises at the prestigious engineering school. Under Jackson's leadership, RPI has become one of the top fifty universities in the United States.

nuclear power plants around the world. During her four-year term with the NRC, Jackson traveled to twenty-eight different countries to assist with nuclear policies. Jackson was asked to serve a second term with the NRC, but then she was offered the presidency of Rensselaer Polytechnic Institute in Troy, New York. She says she could not resist the opportunity to return to academia in a way that gave her the chance to shape an entire educational institution and "craft a vision for the institute for the future."[52]

Continuing Contributions

Since 1999 Jackson has been the president of Rensselaer Polytechnic Institute, and she has turned it into a world-class institution. The university is ranked as one of the top fifty universities nationwide, and research goals are ongoing, according to the university's Office of the President, "to address the greatest challenges of humanity in energy, water, and food security; national and global security; human health; climate change; and the allocation of scarce natural resources."[53]

In addition, Jackson continues to be involved in public policy initiatives. In 2014 President Barack Obama appointed her to be the cochair of his Intelligence Advisory Board. She also advises the secretary of state and the secretary of energy. Today it is reasonable to say that Shirley Ann Jackson really did become "Shirley the Great."

CHAPTER 6

Rosalind W. Picard

Rosalind Wright Picard knows that she was born in Boston, Massachusetts, on May 17, 1962, but she never knew her biological parents. She knows only that her biological mother was a teenager who had an accidental pregnancy. Nevertheless, she is grateful that the young woman gave her the gift of life, and she says, "I was adopted by wonderful parents."[54] Her adoptive parents always told her they would support her in whatever she wanted to do. They encouraged her curiosity and taught her a love of learning. Rosalind's father was a navy pilot, and that meant that the family moved around a lot while she was growing up.

A Multifaceted Youth

When Picard recalls her teen years, she describes herself as not a particularly good student. She was interested in boys and having fun and in learning to skydive. She cut classes. Her school did not have a very good science program, which was part of the problem: Rosalind liked science and math. Her parents finally enrolled her in a nearby science center program a couple afternoons a week. There, Rosalind learned about electricity, electronics, and building things. Her father also enrolled her in YMCA classes to learn about how car engines work and how to tune up an automobile. Rosalind and her father often worked on the family cars together—and nobody ever criticized her for having grease under her fingernails or for taking an interest in science and math.

From her mother, who was a teacher, Rosalind learned to love art and literature as well as activities such as sewing, cooking, design, and shopping. Picard recalls, "Mom encouraged me to conduct a proper manicure, painting my nails to hide those last bits of grease that were hard to wash away."[55] Picard credits both of her parents for letting her know that whatever she wanted out of life was what they wanted for her.

Engineering and Computers

When she graduated from high school, Picard entered the Georgia Institute of Technology, where she decided to major in engineering, mostly because she was told that engineers get good starting salaries and have financially successful careers. She loved electrical engineering and was an excellent student. She graduated from Georgia Tech with highest honors in 1984. She had become very interested in learning to design computer chips, so she went to work at AT&T Bell Laboratories, where she could research chip design. This research got her interested in how human brains work as she tried to make computers think more like people. She entered the Massachusetts Institute of Technology (MIT) and earned a master's degree in 1986 and then a doctorate in 1991 in both electrical engineering and computer science. At that point she joined the MIT Media Lab as a member of the faculty and began the research that would become her lifelong profession.

The Media Lab is a group of creative researchers who study and invent digital technologies that interface and interact with people. Their work is varied; it involves twenty-four research groups involved in more than 350 different projects in areas such as robotics, computers, wearable technology, digital treatments for neurological disorders, electric cars, and video and graphic design. Picard was researching artificial intelligence (AI) and trying to learn ways to make computers function more like human brains. She was building mathematical models to enhance a computer's perceptions (such as sight and hearing) and enable these functions to perform as they do in humans. Like most computer researchers, she believed that AI should imitate the higher functions of the human cortex—where logic, reasoning, and decision making occur.

As she continued her study, however, Picard came to realize that emotion is an integral part of decision making and

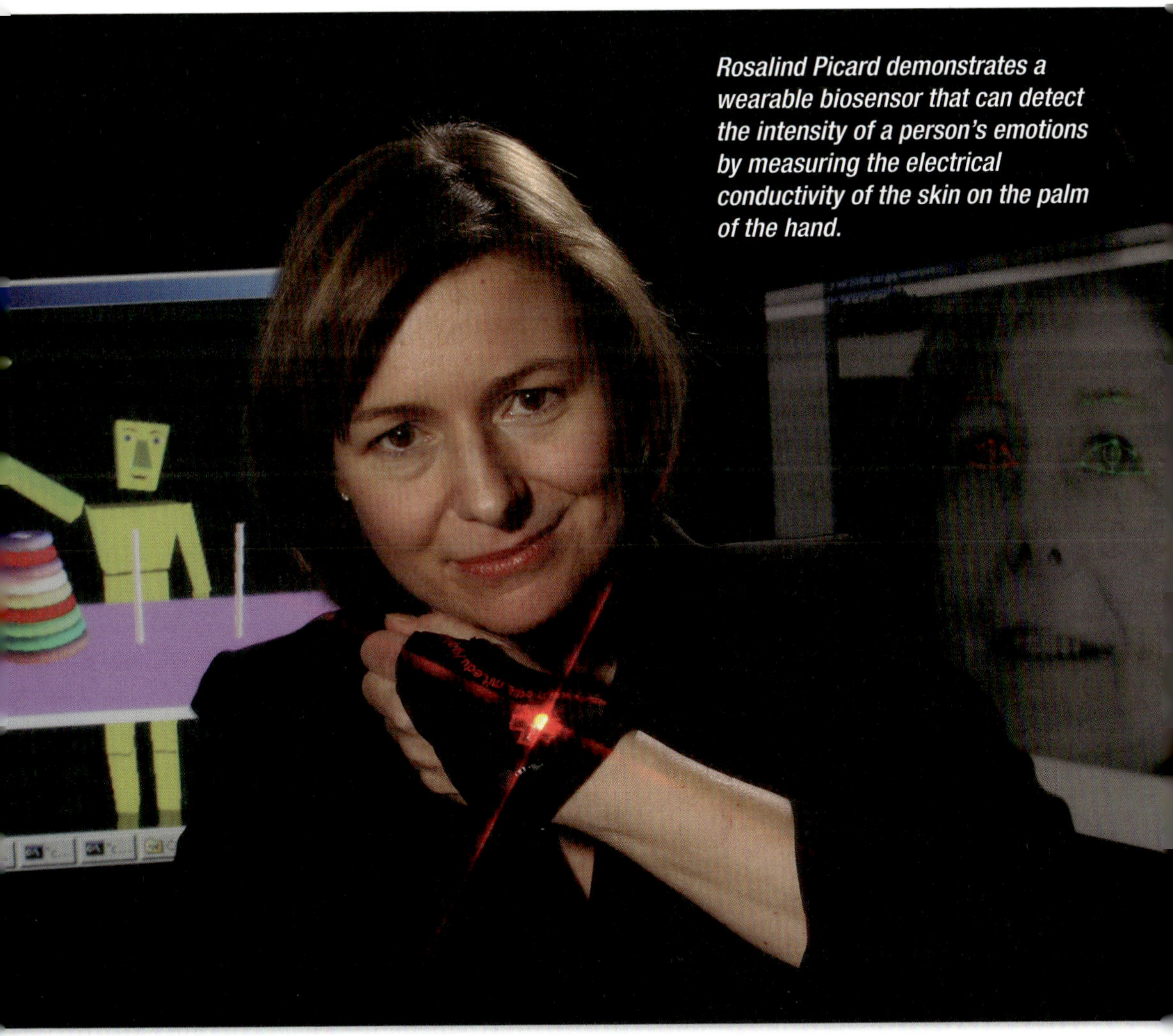

Rosalind Picard demonstrates a wearable biosensor that can detect the intensity of a person's emotions by measuring the electrical conductivity of the skin on the palm of the hand.

rational thought in people. The more primitive parts of the human brain—especially the limbic system, where emotions arise—are as much a part of human thought and perceptions and of social interactions as the cortex. Picard read a book called *The Man Who Tasted Shapes* by neurologist Richard Cytowic. The book describes a condition known as synesthesia in which senses seem to be confused, and people say they can hear colors as well as see them or feel the things they taste as different shapes. Picard was fascinated by the realization that different parts of the brain affect experiences, perceptions, and reasoning in extremely complex ways. She became convinced that without emotion, AI could never even approximate human intelligence. It was not a popular conclusion. It seemed weird and unscientific. Nobody thought emotions were worth studying; emotions just got in the way of reason and logic.

Taking the Emotional Leap

Picard worried about following this course of study. She was young, blonde, and good looking—and she was trying to succeed in a mostly male scientific field. If she pursued investigations into emotion, she feared she would lose the respect of her colleagues and ruin her career. She remembers thinking, "Look, I'm a woman in science. I am not touching emotion." Yet, the more she researched neuroscience, the more she became convinced that emotion plays a critical role in intelligence. "So I faced this dilemma, do I muddy my name by dealing with emotion or do I keep ignoring what the evidence is saying and just do what everybody in my field is doing?"[56] she recalls. She decided to take the risk and jump into a subject no one else had considered—technology should be able to use and interpret emotion.

> "So I faced this dilemma, do I muddy my name by dealing with emotion or do I keep ignoring what the evidence is saying and just do what everybody in my field is doing?"[56]
>
> *—Rosalind Picard*

Family Life

Rosalind W. Picard met Len Picard, her husband of twenty-three years, at MIT, and today they live in Newton, Massachusetts, with their three sons. She says her husband is wonderful and amazing and that her sons "are truly the best boys on the planet." The family lives a normal life, and none of their computers are affective. Sometimes her younger sons have been interested in wearing biosensor wristbands, but, she says, as the boys get older they do not want to be seen wearing anything that looks weird or uncool. For the most part, Picard keeps her research firmly in the MIT labs.

Rosalind Picard, "Will Technology Save the World?," Readable. www.allreadable.com.

Picard came up with the term *affective computing* to describe her research into how technology could be used to recognize and interpret emotion and how emotions could be quantified and measured. She began to give talks to other engineers and computer scientists about what affective computing is and why the study of emotions matters. She wrote scientific articles about affective computing, and in 1997 she wrote a book about the subject. In the beginning, she says, "I learned people are uncomfortable with emotion. They didn't think that it could be serious science. And they really didn't know anything about it. And I hear them say stuff like, 'She used to work on respectable stuff. What happened?' . . . There was a lot of rejection."[57]

Measuring Emotion with Sensors

Gradually, however, Picard's science won over the doubters. Today she is credited with developing a new field of scientific study. At the Media Lab, she is the head of the Affective Computing research group, and along with her team of graduate students and her computer scientist colleague Rana el Kaliouby, she has been responsible for important breakthroughs in computer research. At first the team concentrated on teaching computers to have emotional intelligence—to recognize when people felt angry or pleased in their computer interactions. In the late 1990s the two developed a squeezable mouse with pressure sensors inside that could detect a person's tension level. It was used with Microsoft's onscreen assistant, known as Clippy. Writer Adam Higginbotham gives an example of how it worked. He explains, "In one demonstration a student tried to address a letter to a Mr Abotu, a name the software repeatedly insisted on changing to 'Mr About.' As the software registered the student's grip tightening in fury, Clippy appeared and observed, 'It seems as if you're frustrated. Should I turn off AutoCorrect?'"[58] This is emotional intelligence: a com-

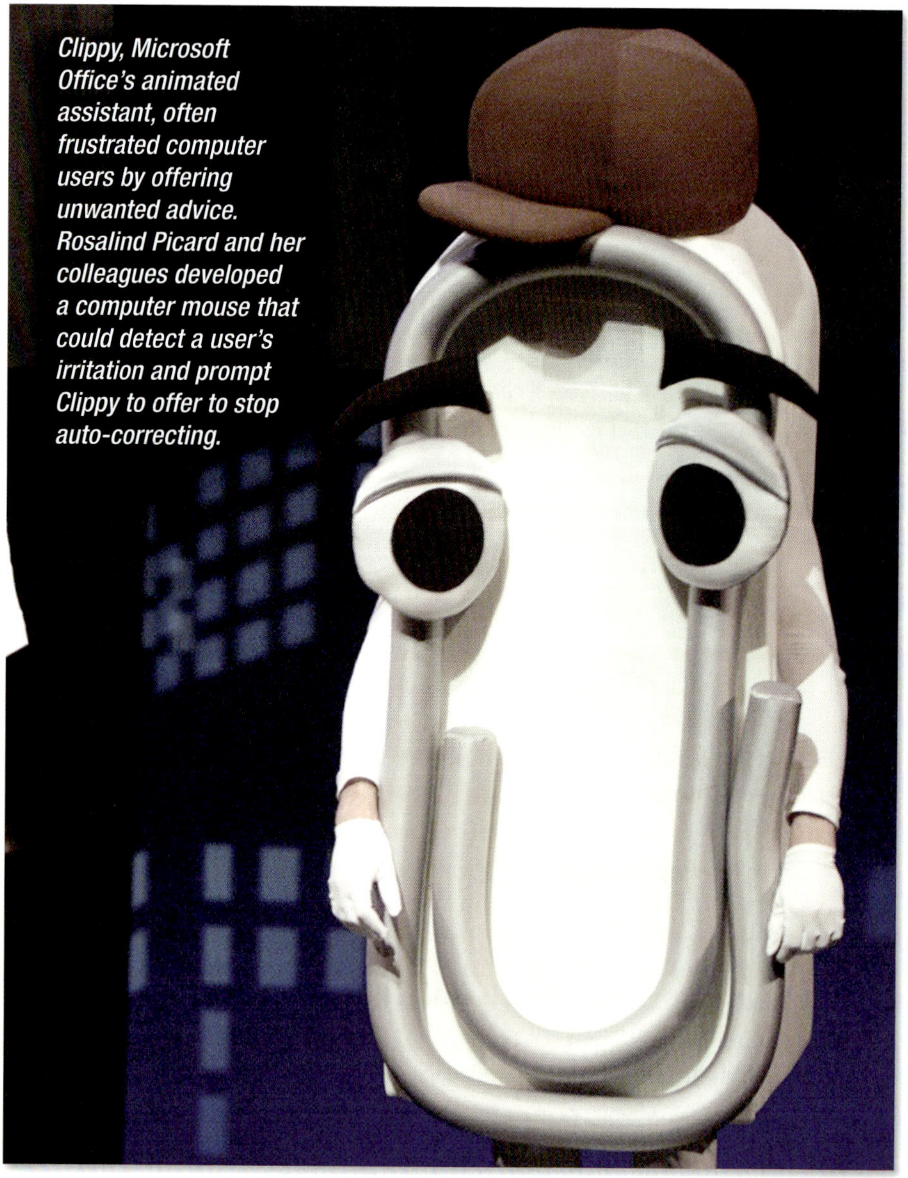

Clippy, Microsoft Office's animated assistant, often frustrated computer users by offering unwanted advice. Rosalind Picard and her colleagues developed a computer mouse that could detect a user's irritation and prompt Clippy to offer to stop auto-correcting.

puter's ability to detect and respond appropriately to a human emotion. The team also invented other technology for detecting emotions. They came up with glasses that could detect a frown on a human face, a hat with an attached camera that could read facial expressions, and a glove that could measure sweating in the skin that increases with emotional arousal.

Eventually these developments led to the invention of wearable biosensors—headbands and wristbands that can be worn for weeks at a time and continually measure electrical skin responses and other physiological signs of emotional arousal. The team named these devices Q Sensors. The biosensors stream data to a computer or store it for later download and measure emotional reactions to daily activities. The Q Sensors turned out to have important implications for children with autism. People with autism can have a hard time understanding and expressing emotion. Many autistic children are nonverbal, and they often have meltdowns or tantrums for no discernible reason, even after seeming calm and unresponsive only moments before. Picard's Q Sensors reveal a different story. The data from a wearable biosensor shows that a calm-appearing child is actually experiencing increasing levels of stress. The overload is too much for an extremely sensitive autistic child. The child shuts down in response and appears calm on the outside, but then the stress becomes too much, leading to a meltdown. It is not without reason at all; the child simply cannot describe or express his or her distress. If caregivers know that a child is experiencing rising stress—perhaps, for example, from a loud TV program—they can remove the stress and thus prevent many meltdowns. Picard devised a method to stream wristband data to a cell phone carried by a parent or caregiver. In this way, an autistic child's true emotions can be identified and understood. Picard explains, "The sensors have provided data that has allowed people to see things that they were guessing about, and often guessing wrong."[59]

"The sensors have provided data that has allowed people to see things that they were guessing about, and often guessing wrong."[59]

—Rosalind Picard

Q Sensors turned out to have wide applications in a number of areas. The team discovered that spikes in the data from wristbands could predict seizures 94 percent of the time in children with epilepsy who were wearing the devices. Likewise, advertisers could use them to measure people's responses to commercials and find out what types of messages provoke positive responses to their products. Picard has worn one of her sensors most of the time for several years and believes that they have helped her understand her own emotions better. She says, "You realize that these devices measure a feeling you've had your whole life that you don't know the name of. It's the feeling of your hands getting sweaty before something. It's the feeling of something that matters happening."[60]

Affective Computing Success

Interest in affective computing and wearable biosensors exploded. Picard has achieved international recognition for her work, including numerous awards and appointments to several science and engineering program committees. She has written or cowritten more than two hundred scientific papers about affective computing and is a sought-after guest speaker at universities and professional conferences. She holds multiple patents for inventions of wearable and nonwearable biosensors and computer systems that sense and respond to human emotional information. The field of affective computing has its own scientific journal and its own international annual conference and professional society. No one questions Picard's scientific credibility anymore.

In 2011 Picard partnered with Italian businessman Matteo Lai to launch the affective computing company Empatica. It has developed and produced the E4 wristband for clinical research and scientific monitoring. The E4 allows continuous data monitoring of physiological responses in the wearer. It stores the data and can stream information on a cloud platform or download data via computer or a smartphone app. Some of the companies using the technology include Intel, NASA, Sony, and Boston Children's

Faith and Science Together

Picard says that she was raised without any religion, but now as an adult she is firm in her Christian faith. She explains,

> I was a proud atheist. I thought that rational scientific thinking was the only way an intelligent person would operate, and I assumed it was sufficient for all truth. . . . [But] Science and faith are more than compatible—they are complementary, like two wings to lift us off the ground and help us see more than we can down here. In science, we tend to not speak of faith—but we speak of experience, intuition, hunches, ideas, imagination, and inklings, all of which can be informed by science's experiments, but never is all of our action and decision based entirely on the latter or entirely upon proven truths. All scientists practice faith of some kind.

Quoted in Alison Hull, "Big Interview—April 2010—Scientist Ros Picard," *Inspire.* www.inspiremagazine.org.uk.

Hospital. Empatica is also preparing to introduce its newest wristband sensor—called Embrace—to the general public sometime in 2016. Embrace is wearable technology, like a smartwatch, but it has medical-grade quality. It is sleek and comfortable to wear, and it can continuously monitor seizure activity, sleep activity, stress levels, and physical activity. It is equipped with a wristband notification system to warn the user if stress levels are rising or seizure activity is noted. It has an alert app for the wearer's smartphone. The Empatica website explains about the watch, "You can check your entire day in a glance in a way that is easy to understand. Not only during exercise, but also at work, during your commute, during the night. If you push yourself too much, the Embrace watch will gently remind you with a vibration, that you need some time to recover. You can customize it to suit your needs and behavior."[61]

For the Good of Everyone

Picard has high hopes that technology like Embrace will improve people's lives, not only for those who experience seizures or have autism but also for anyone who wants to understand how stress and emotions affect their health. She says that a future smartwatch will teach people more about emotions. "Consumers," she adds, "will have fun seeing things that make their stress levels go up and down. Yes, it goes up with music recitals, bullying, driving and arguments. But it also goes up with things that are fun and exciting. It's real objective data, and you can see what calms a child with autism who is non-speaking or what stresses out your spouse. It's very eye-opening."[62]

> **"It's real objective data, and you can see what calms a child with autism who is non-speaking or what stresses out your spouse. It's very eye-opening."[62]**
>
> *—Rosalind Picard*

But Picard does not think technology is only for fun. She adds, "Ultimately all the technology we build is in service to people. To enable people to live better lives. To allow the human race to be something greater than it has been in the past."[63] She continues to work toward that goal every day.

SOURCE NOTES

Introduction: Awe-Inspiring Contributions

1. Rosalind Chait Barnett and Laura Sabbatini, "A Short History of Women in Science: From Stone Walls to Invisible Walls," Brandeis University, 2009, p. 8. www.brandeis.edu.
2. Quoted in Suzanne Gould, "This Brilliant Female Physicist Was Overlooked for a Nobel Prize," American Association of University Women, September 11, 2013. www.aauw.org.

Chapter 1: Lise Meitner

3. Quoted in Ruth Lewin Sime, *Lise Meitner: A Life in Physics.* Berkeley and Los Angeles: University of California Press, 1996, p. 1.
4. Quoted in Sime, *Lise Meitner*, p. 45.
5. Quoted in Klaus Hoffman, *Otto Hahn: Achievement and Responsibility,* trans. J. Michael Cole. New York: Springer, 2001, p.123.
6. Quoted in Sime, *Lise Meitner*, p. 305.
7. Quoted in Priyamvada Natarajan, "The Myth of the 'Jewish Mother of the Bomb,'" CNN, August 9, 2013. www.cnn.com.
8. Quoted in Sime, *Lise Meitner*, p. 338.
9. Quoted in William H. Cropper, *Great Physicists: The Life and Times of Leading Physicists from Galileo to Hawking.* New York: Oxford University Press, 2004, p. 343.

Chapter 2: Pearl Kendrick

10. Tim Anderson, "Pearl Kendrick: Developed Vaccine That Whoops Whooping Cough!," ScienceHeroes.com. www.scienceheroes.com.
11. Quoted in Carolyn G. Shapiro-Shapin, "Pearl Kendrick, Grace Eldering, and the Pertussis Vaccine," *Emerging Infectious Diseases,* vol. 16, no. 8, August 2010, pp. 1273–78. www.ncbi.nlm.nih.gov.
12. Quoted in Carolyn G. Shapiro-Shapin, "'A Whole Community Working Together': Pearl Kendrick, Grace Eldering, and the Grand Rapids Pertussis Trials, 1932–1939," *Advantage Health Grand Rapids* (blog), 2012. http://advantagehealthgrandrapidshere.blogspot.com.
13. Quoted in Harry Milton Marks, "The Kendrick-Eldering-(Frost) Pertussis Vaccine Field Trial," *James Lind Library Bulletin*, 2006. www.jameslindlibrary.org.
14. Quoted in Marks, "The Kendrick-Eldering-(Frost) Pertussis Vaccine Field Trial."
15. Pearl Kendrick and Grace Eldering, "Cough Plate Examinations for *B. Pertussis*," *American Journal of Public Health,* vol. 24, no. 4, April 1934, p. 318. www.ncbi.nlm.nih.gov.
16. Quoted in Anderson, "Pearl Kendrick."
17. Quoted in Connie Tegge, "Pearl Kendrick—a Woman Who Fought Whooping Cough," *Ann Arbor (MI) News,* February 7, 1971. http//oldnews.aadl.org.

Chapter 3: Virginia Apgar

18. Quoted in Marion Hunt, "Virginia Apgar: Savior of New Lives," in *Living Legacies at Columbia,* ed. Wm. Theodore de Bary with Jerry Kisslinger and Tom Mathewson. New York: Columbia University Press, 2006, p. 256.
19. Quoted in Profiles in Science, "The Virginia Apgar Papers: Biographical Information," National Library of Medicine. http://profiles.nlm.nih.gov.
20. Quoted in Melinda Beck, "How's Your Baby? Recalling the Apgar Score's Namesake," *Wall Street Journal,* May 26, 2009. www.wsj.com.
21. Hunt, "Virginia Apgar," p. 259.

22. Quoted in Hunt, "Virginia Apgar," p. 259.
23. Quoted in Beck, "How's Your Baby?"
24. Quoted in Selma Harrison Calmes, "And What About the Baby? Virginia Apgar and the Apgar Score," *American Society of Anesthesiologists Newsletter,* vol. 61, no. 9, September 1997, p. 21. www.woodlibrarymuseum.org.
25. Quoted in Profiles in Science, "The Virginia Apgar Papers: Obstetric Anesthesia and a Scorecard for Newborns, 1949–1958," National Library of Medicine. http://profiles.nlm.nih.gov.
26. David Rose, "Virginia Apgar," March of Dimes, May 28, 2009. www.marchofdimes.org.
27. Quoted in Hunt, "Virginia Apgar," p. 259.
28. Quoted in Hunt, "Virginia Apgar," p. 261.
29. David Rose, "A History of the March of Dimes," March of Dimes, August 26, 2010. www.marchofdimes.org.
30. Quoted in Beck, "How's Your Baby?"
31. Profiles in Science, "The Virginia Apgar Papers: Biographical Information."

Chapter 4: Jane Goodall

32. Quoted in Jane Goodall, *Africa in My Blood: An Autobiography in Letters: The Early Years*, ed. Dale Peterson. New York: Houghton Mifflin, 2000, p. 4.
33. Quoted in Abigail Jones, "Jane Goodall's Jungles," *Newsweek,* October 23, 2014. www.newsweek.com.
34. Goodall, *Africa in My Blood*, p. 88.
35. Quoted in Robin McKie, "Chimps with Everything: Jane Goodall's 50 Years in the Jungle," *Guardian*, June 26, 2010. www.theguardian.com.
36. Goodall, *Africa in My Blood*, p. 172.
37. Quoted in David Quammen, "Fifty Years at Gombe," *National Geographic*, October 2010. http://ngm.nationalgeographic.com.
38. Goodall, *Africa in My Blood*, p. 186.
39. Jane Goodall, *Through a Window: My Thirty Years with the Chimpanzees of Gombe.* New York: Mariner, 2010, p. 300.
40. Quoted in Paul Tullis, "Jane Goodall Is Still Wild at Heart," *New York Times Magazine,* March 13, 2015. www.nytimes.com.

41. Quoted in National Geographic, "Explorers: Jane Goodall." www.nationalgeographic.com.

Chapter 5: Shirley Ann Jackson

42. Quoted in Joan Oleck, "Contemporary Black Biography: Shirley Ann Jackson," Encyclopedia.com, 1996. www.encyclopedia.com.
43. Quoted in *Q&A,* "Q&A with Shirley Ann Jackson," C-SPAN, December 10, 2004. www.c-span.org.
44. Quoted in HistoryMakers, "Shirley Ann Jackson," HistoryMakers TEST ScienceMakers Video Archive, session 1, tape 3, story 3. www.idvl.org.
45. Quoted in HistoryMakers, "Shirley Ann Jackson," session 1, tape 3, story 6.
46. Quoted in Oleck, "Contemporary Black Biography."
47. Quoted in Nancy Connell, "Aim for the Stars," *Rensselaer Magazine,* September 1999. http://rpi.edu.
48. Scott W. Williams, "Physicists of the African Diaspora: Shirley Ann Jackson," State University of New York at Buffalo. www.math.buffalo.edu.
49. Quoted in Oleck, "Contemporary Black Biography."
50. Oleck, "Contemporary Black Biography."
51. Quoted in HistoryMakers, "Shirley Ann Jackson," HistoryMakers TEST ScienceMakers Video Archive, session 2, tape 12, story 1.
52. Quoted in HistoryMakers, "Shirley Ann Jackson," HistoryMakers TEST ScienceMakers Video Archive, session 2, tape 13, story 3.
53. Office of the President, "Profile of Shirley Ann Jackson, Ph.D," Rensselaer Polytechnic Institute. http://rpi.edu.

Chapter 6: Rosalind W. Picard

54. Quoted in *Cambridge Nights,* "Rosalind Picard—on Life," season 2, November 5, 2012. www.cambridgenights.com.
55. Rosalind Wright Picard, "Tribute to My Parents on Their 50th Wedding Anniversary," Rosalind Picard Personal Page, MIT Media Lab. http://web.media.mit.edu.
56. Quoted in *Cambridge Nights,* "Rosalind Picard."
57. Quoted in Sigma Xi, "An Interview with Rosalind W. Picard: Adding Emotion to Computing," December 12, 2014. www.sigmaxi.org.

58. Adam Higginbotham, "Welcome to Rosalind Picard's Touchy-Feely World of Empathic Tech," *Wired,* November 27, 2012. www.wired.co.uk.
59. Quoted in Arthur Allen, "Feeling Mad? New Devices Can Sense Your Mood and Tell—or Even Text—Others," *Washington Post,* January 13, 2014. www.washingtonpost.com.
60. Quoted in Allen, "Feeling Mad?"
61. Empatica, "Embrace Watch." http://store.empatica.com.
62. Quoted in Joao Medeiros, "Embrace Is the Medical-Grade Wearable We've Been Waiting For," *Wired,* November 19, 2014. www.wired.co.uk.
63. Quoted in Wendy Jewell, "Science Hero: Rosalind Picard," My Hero Project, March 21, 2015. http://myhero.com.

FOR FURTHER RESEARCH

Books

Winifred Conkling, *Radioactive! How Irène Curie and Lise Meitner Revolutionized Science and Changed the World*. Chapel Hill, NC: Algonquin Young Readers, 2016.

Andi Diehn, *Technology: Cool Women Who Code.* White River Junction, VT: Nomad, 2015.

Vicki V. May, *Engineering: Cool Women Who Design.* White River Junction, VT: Nomad, 2016.

Penny Noyce, *Remarkable Minds: 17 More Pioneering Women in Science and Medicine.* Boston: Tumblehome Learning, 2015.

Diane O'Connell, *Strong Force: The Story of Physicist Shirley Ann Jackson.* Washington, DC: National Academies, 2006.

Jim Ottaviani, *Primates: The Fearless Science of Jane Goodall, Dian Fossey, and Birutė Galdikas.* New York: First Second, 2013.

Websites

EngineerGirl (www.engineergirl.org). This site, sponsored by the National Academy of Engineering, is dedicated to describing the opportunities for girls and women in engineering careers. It offers stories about female engineers, descriptions of different engineering careers, educational advice, contests, and much more.

Famous Female Scientists (http://famousfemalescientists.com). This site offers biographies of fourteen different women scientists in various fields.

Famous Women Inventors (www.women-inventors.com). Learn about the contributions of women inventors, what they did, and how they achieved their results.

The Jane Goodall Institute (www.janegoodall.org). Jane Goodall's institute has an extensive website that includes stories about Goodall, descriptions of the institute's work, and the ways in which everyone can get involved with her ongoing work.

Profiles in Science (http://profiles.nlm.nih.gov). This website of the US National Library of Medicine profiles the twentieth-century men and women who have made significant contributions to biomedical research and public health.

INDEX

Note: Boldface page numbers indicate illustrations.

PICTURE CREDITS

Cover: © Photoshot

6: © NIAID-NIH/PHANIE/phanie/Phanie Sarl/Corbis

10: Portrait of Lisa Meitner (1878–1968) (b/w photo)/Private Collection/ Prismatic Pictures/Bridgeman Images

15: © Bettmann/Corbis

20: Colorized by Maury Aaseng

25: © Michael Owen Baker/ZUMA Press/Corbis

31: Science Source

34: Library of Congress/Science Photo Library

41: Associated Press

45: © Michel Gunther/Minden Pictures

50: Emilio Segre Visual Archives/American Institute of Physics/Science Photo Library

55: © Tim Roske/AP/Corbis

59: © Rick Friedman/Corbis

62: © Reuters/Corbis

ABOUT THE AUTHOR

Toney Allman holds degrees from Ohio State University and the University of Hawaii. She currently lives in Virginia, where she enjoys a rural lifestyle as well as researching and writing about a variety of topics for students.